WILMA WADE MYSTERIES

VOLUME 2

DAISY LANDISH

BEACHES AND TRAILS
PUBLISHING

MURDER AT THE PARADE

A SMALL-TOWN EASTER COZY MYSTERY WITH A SENIOR SLEUTH

CHAPTER ONE

WILMA WADE TUGGED at the edges of the Easter Bunny suit, scowling at her reflection in the full-length mirror. The oversized white costume swallowed her, the pink-lined ears flopping to the sides instead of standing upright. A massive blue bow sat crooked at the collar, and the mittens made her hands look like swollen clouds. The worst of it sat in the chair beside her—the ridiculous mascot head, its stitched-on grin mocking her. It was one of those absurd hat-like heads that would show her head beneath the rabbit face. Maybe it wouldn't be so bad if it was fully enclosed, but everyone would recognize her in this suit.

She exhaled sharply and muttered, "I must have been blackmailed."

A voice from the doorway answered, "No, you were guilted, which is much more effective."

Wilma turned to find Maggie Trent, the town's Easter Parade coordinator, leaning against the doorframe, clipboard in hand, an expression of pure amusement on her face.

"This is the last time I let Wanda Carter ambush me at the bakery," Wilma grumbled, adjusting the itchy fabric at her wrists.

"One minute, I'm buying a loaf of sourdough, and the next, I'm being told I'll ruin Easter if I don't 'volunteer.'"

"She's a master of persuasion." Maggie checked something off her list. "And now here you are, Barwick's very own Easter Bunny."

Wilma sighed, glaring at her reflection. "I was hoping to enjoy the parade from the sidewalk this year, watching the floats, sampling cookies, like a normal person. Not sweating in a rabbit suit."

Maggie waved a dismissive hand. "You'll be fine. You just have to walk down Main Street handing out candy. Maybe pose for a few pictures with the kids at the park afterward. No one expects you to hop."

Wilma shot her a dark look. "If anyone asks me to hop, I'm resigning from Easter."

Maggie smirked. "I'll be sure to make that announcement."

Before Wilma could come up with a suitably scathing reply, the door swung open wider and Detective Jason Fellow stepped in. He stopped in his tracks, eyes landing on the costume, then shifting to Wilma's face.

His lips pressed together, fighting the unmistakable twitch of amusement.

Wilma pointed a fuzzy white mitten at him. "Say one word, and you're off my Christmas cookie list."

Jason coughed into his fist. "Wouldn't dream of it."

Maggie grinned. "Come on, Jason. She looks fantastic."

Wilma huffed. "I look like an overgrown stuffed animal."

Jason tilted his head. "Festive."

Maggie snorted.

Wilma crossed her arms, as best she could in the bulky suit. "If you weren't here on police business, I'd make you wear this instead."

Jason smirked. "You'd have to catch me first."

Wilma narrowed her eyes, but before she could fire back,

Maggie checked her watch. "Parade starts in twenty minutes. Wilma, you're leading the lineup as planned. Tom Alden's in place as Grand Marshal. Bake sale is already in full swing. We're set."

Wilma relaxed slightly at the mention of Tom. "How's he doing? He seemed a little… preoccupied when I saw him earlier."

Jason's expression shifted. "Preoccupied how?"

Wilma frowned. "Nothing specific. Just not his usual self."

Maggie waved a hand. "It's probably business. Running a garage and car lot keeps him busy."

Jason nodded. "Tom's been a pillar of Barwick forever. Hard to imagine anything rattling him."

Wilma wasn't sure about that, but before she could dwell on it, Maggie clapped her hands. "Alright, Bunny. Get your head on. You're up in five."

Wilma glared at the grinning rabbit head, then reached for it with a sigh.

She had a very bad feeling about today.

––––––––

Wilma stepped out of the Barwick Community Center, the bright spring sunshine momentarily blinding her. The warmth was deceptive—beneath the cheerful Easter decorations, a cool breeze cut through the town square, carrying the scent of freshly baked goods from the nearby bake sale.

She adjusted the oversized rabbit hat on her head and surveyed the scene. Families lined the sidewalks, children clutching colorful baskets, their eyes darting excitedly toward the parade lineup. Vendors manned tables laden with Easter-themed cookies, cupcakes, and pies, while volunteers directed last-minute float adjustments. The high school marching band stood at the ready, their brass instruments gleaming in the sun.

Wilma almost enjoyed the lively energy—if not for the absurd costume and the promise of public embarrassment.

"Miss Wade!"

She turned to see Lena Morgan, her apron dusted with flour, hurrying over from the bake sale stall. She carried a small, foil-wrapped chocolate egg in her flour-covered hands.

"For you," Lena said cheerfully, pressing it into Wilma's palm.

Wilma raised a brow. "Bribing the Easter Bunny?"

Lena laughed. "Consider it a thank-you for keeping tradition alive."

Wilma glanced at the egg, then slipped it into her Easter basket for later. "Well, you're making sure half the town gets a sugar rush, so I'd say you're doing more for tradition than I am."

Lena beamed. "It's the busiest bake sale we've had in years. If we keep this up, we'll actually hit our fundraising goal for the community center renovations."

"That's wonderful," Wilma said, then noticed Lena glancing toward the parade lineup, her fingers absently twisting the strings of her apron.

"Everything alright?" Wilma asked.

Lena hesitated. "I just… saw Tom Alden earlier. He was looking a little pale, don't you think?"

Wilma's brow furrowed. "I thought so too. Did he say anything to you?"

"Not really. Just seemed off," Lena said. "I thought maybe he wasn't feeling well, but you know Tom—he'd never admit it."

Wilma nodded. Tom Alden was not the type to complain, not even when something was clearly bothering him. She tucked the thought away for later.

As she made her way toward the parade lineup, the crowd thickened. Small children darted between parents' legs, their baskets already half-full from the early candy handouts. The hum of conversation mixed with the distant notes of the marching band warming up.

Wilma spotted Tom Alden standing beside his cherry-red convertible, chatting with a few town council members. He was dressed sharply in a light-blue suit, a departure from his usual work attire.

"Wilma!" he called, spotting her.

She waddled over, adjusting the plush mittens on her hands. "Tom, you clean up well."

He chuckled, but it was weaker than usual. "And you look... fluffy."

She sighed. "The entire town seems to agree."

Tom grinned, but then, just for a moment, a shadow passed over his face. He shifted slightly, lowering his voice. "Hey, if something happens—"

Wilma's stomach dropped. "Something happens?"

Tom hesitated, shaking his head quickly. "Never mind. It's just —" He exhaled, rubbing his temple. "Guess I'm just getting old."

Wilma didn't buy it.

"Tom," she said, lowering her own voice, "if something's wrong, you can tell me."

But before he could answer, Maggie blew her whistle, signaling for everyone to take their places.

"Gotta go," Tom said, flashing a half-hearted smile as he climbed into the convertible. "See you at the finish line."

Wilma watched him go, a deep unease settling in her chest.

Something wasn't right. And she had the awful feeling she was about to find out exactly what.

———

The Barwick Easter Parade began with the steady rhythm of drums, the high school marching band setting the tempo as the first float rolled forward. Children cheered, waving small paper flags, while parents leaned into their folding chairs, soaking in the warm spring air.

Wilma walked the route, doing her best to move smoothly despite the cumbersome Easter Bunny costume, passing out candy to eager little hands reaching up toward her. She was already too warm inside the thick suit, her breath trapped in the oversized head.

The scent of fresh-baked pastries from the bake sale stalls drifted along the street, mingling with the crisp scent of fresh flowers from the floats. A few vendors had set up small booths along the sidewalk, selling handmade crafts, knitted bunnies, and festive Easter wreaths.

From his cherry-red convertible, Tom Alden rode ahead, smiling as he tossed tiny bags of jellybeans to the kids.

Despite the cheerful atmosphere, Wilma's unease only deepened.

She kept stealing glances at Tom. Something was wrong. He was still smiling, but it looked more forced now, as if it required effort to keep up. The usual brightness in his eyes was missing.

Then he stiffened, just slightly, before shaking his head as if trying to clear his thoughts.

Wilma slowed her pace.

A moment later, Tom's hand faltered mid-wave. His fingers twitched, hesitated, then clutched at his chest.

Wilma stopped walking.

Tom's face twisted into something unreadable. He sucked in a sharp breath and pitched forward, barely catching himself on the edge of the windshield.

For a moment, no one reacted. The crowd continued to cheer, oblivious. The marching band played on, their brass notes soaring through the air.

Then, Tom collapsed against the steering wheel.

Gasps rippled through the crowd.

The convertible continued rolling forward, moving slowly along the street, but Tom's weight pushing against the wheel sent the vehicle slightly off course.

Wilma's breath caught in her throat.

Jason Fellow, standing near the judging table, was already

moving. His tall frame cut through the crowd as he sprinted toward the car, his hands reaching for the driver's side door before anyone else could react.

A child screamed. Parents pulled their kids back from the street. The laughter and cheers that had filled Main Street moments ago had evaporated into a stunned, hushed silence.

Wilma tore off the rabbit head, the cool air rushing against her damp skin.

She ran forward, her heartbeat hammering in her chest.

Jason shook Tom's shoulder. "Tom!" His voice was sharp, demanding.

Tom didn't move.

Jason swore under his breath, his eyes scanning Tom's face, his ashen skin, his unmoving chest. He reached for his radio, barking orders for medical assistance, but Wilma already knew—

Tom wasn't going to wake up.

She stared at his lifeless body, her mind catching on one terrible, gut-deep realization.

Tom Alden was dead. And whatever had just happened to him hadn't been natural.

CHAPTER TWO

THE JOYFUL BUZZ of the Easter parade had evaporated, replaced by a low hum of confusion, fear, and disbelief. Parents clutched their children close, shielding their eyes from the sight of Tom Alden's lifeless body slumped in his convertible. Others stood frozen, their hands covering their mouths, unable to process what had just happened.

Wilma had seen death before. But never like this. Never in the middle of Main Street, during one of Barwick's most treasured celebrations.

Jason Fellow was already in action, kneeling beside Tom in the driver's seat, fingers searching for a pulse. His jaw was tight, his face grim. A long, tense moment passed before he looked up and shook his head.

"He's gone," Jason said, his voice flat.

A murmur rippled through the crowd. Some gasped. Others whispered in disbelief.

From the back of the parade lineup, Maggie Trent, still gripping her clipboard, took a half-step forward, as if trying to will the situation into something less terrible. "But—but he was fine. He was waving. He was—" Her voice cracked.

Wilma swallowed the lump in her throat and took a slow step forward, her gaze locked onto Tom's motionless hand, draped over the side of the car. It looked... unnatural. Limp, like a discarded glove.

A shrill voice cut through the murmur. "Somebody call an ambulance!"

"I already did," Jason said, pushing himself up from his crouch. His eyes met Wilma's for half a second, and she recognized the look in them. It was the same look he had when they'd stumbled upon their last unexpected corpse—a mixture of frustration and something darker. Suspicion.

Wilma opened her mouth to speak, but before she could, the sound of sirens pierced the air. The Barwick paramedics arrived in record time, weaving through the crowd with practiced urgency. They moved swiftly, checking for vitals, but Jason's assessment had already been confirmed.

Tom Alden was dead.

The lead paramedic, a tall woman with sharp cheekbones and graying hair, exchanged a look with Jason before pulling him aside. Wilma strained to hear but caught only pieces of their conversation.

"—no immediate injuries—"

"—not a heart attack—"

"—could be poisoning—"

Wilma's stomach turned. Poison?

She took another step closer, her eyes scanning the scene for anything out of place.

And then she saw it.

Near the passenger seat, just beneath Tom's unmoving hand, lay a crumpled pastry wrapper and what looked like a half-eaten cinnamon roll.

Wilma's breath hitched. The bake sale.

She wasn't the only one who saw it. Jason followed her gaze, his expression darkening.

"You see it too?" he murmured.

Wilma nodded slowly. "Looks like he had a snack before the parade."

Jason's eyes flicked back toward Tom's pale face. "His last one."

Wilma glanced at the bakery tent in the distance, where Lena Morgan and the other volunteers stood frozen in place, their aprons still dusted with flour, their faces drained of color.

If the pastry had been poisoned, the question wasn't just who would do such a thing.

The bigger question was why.

————

The paramedics covered Tom's body with a crisp white sheet, and the air around them seemed to still, as if even the town itself was holding its breath. Wilma watched as a few townsfolk turned away, unable to look. Others whispered behind their hands, their faces pale with shock.

The Easter Parade had been officially ruined.

Jason Fellow stood near the convertible, giving quiet instructions to one of his deputies. Within minutes, the area was roped off with yellow tape and the once-joyous energy of the parade route had transformed into something else entirely—a crime scene.

Wilma folded her arms, glancing back at the crowd. Several people lingered, stunned and uneasy, unsure whether to stay and gawk or retreat into their homes, where bad things didn't happen on bright spring mornings.

The sound of footsteps drew her attention.

Dr. Eleanor Granger, the town's medical examiner, arrived with her assistant, carrying a black medical bag. She adjusted her thick glasses, her gray-streaked hair pulled into a neat bun.

Jason gestured toward the body. "Tell me what we've got, Doc."

Dr. Granger crouched beside Tom, peeling back the sheet. She gave his face a brief, clinical examination before moving to his hands, gently lifting one by the wrist.

"No obvious trauma," she murmured. "No contusions, no wounds."

Wilma took a step closer. "Could it be a heart attack?"

Dr. Granger shook her head. "Doubtful. His skin tone is slightly off, but not in the way I'd expect from cardiac arrest. If I had to guess, I'd say toxin exposure."

Jason exhaled sharply, rubbing the back of his neck. "Poison."

Wilma felt her stomach tighten. The word lingered in the air like smoke.

Dr. Granger gave a curt nod. "I'll have to run tests to be certain, but the symptoms match. Sudden collapse, no signs of external struggle. Whatever it was, it acted fast."

Jason muttered a curse under his breath, then turned to his deputies. "I want a full sweep of this area. Start with his car. Anything that looks like food or drink, bag it for evidence."

Wilma's mind was already racing ahead of him. "Did you get the pastry he was eating?" she asked, gesturing toward the convertible. "He must have eaten it right before the parade started."

"It was the first thing I bagged," Jason assured to her.

"We can't assume that it was what was poisoned. It might have been something else," Wilma added, frowning.

Jason nodded his agreement as he gestured toward one of the younger officers, Deputy Carly Reed, who had just finished securing the perimeter. "Carly, bag up any food or drink in the vehicle. And get a sample of everything to Granger for testing."

The deputy nodded and moved quickly toward the convertible.

Wilma turned her attention back to the crowd. People were watching from a distance, their faces uncertain, wary. She had lived in Barwick long enough to know that soon, those whispers would turn into rumors, and the rumors would snowball into accusations.

She caught sight of Lena Morgan, still in her flour-dusted apron, standing with the other bake sale volunteers. Her arms were wrapped around herself, her eyes darting between the convertible and the gathered police.

Wilma wasn't the only one who noticed.

Jason followed her gaze and exhaled sharply. "If that pastry was poisoned, we need to start at the source."

"The bake sale," Wilma murmured.

Jason nodded. "And we need to find out if Tom Alden was the intended victim."

Or, Wilma thought uneasily, was the poison meant for someone else?

———

Jason signaled for his deputies to start questioning the crowd while he turned back to Dr. Granger, who was preparing to have Tom's body transported for a full examination. The rumble of uneasy conversation had settled over Main Street, the town's excitement for the parade entirely replaced by whispers and furtive glances.

Wilma didn't wait for Jason to tell her to stay put—she was already moving.

She made her way toward the bake sale tents, where a few volunteers stood frozen in place, still gripping their trays and utensils as if they'd only just realized something terrible had happened.

Lena Morgan was the first to notice Wilma's approach. She turned, her face pale, hands still coated in a fine layer of flour. "Is… is it true?" she whispered. "Did Tom really…?"

Wilma nodded, keeping her voice low. "He collapsed. Dr. Granger thinks it may have been poisoning."

A ripple of horror and confusion passed through the other bakers.

"Poison?" gasped Irene Holloway, the owner of Barwick's general store, her fingers tightening around the tray of hot cross buns she had been about to serve.

"That's impossible," another baker said, shaking her head. "We made everything fresh this morning."

Wilma glanced at the display table, where rows of cinnamon rolls, lemon bars, carrot cupcakes, and cookies sat untouched now, the festive pastel tablecloth fluttering slightly in the breeze.

A terrible thought crept into her mind.

Jason joined them a moment later, his boots crunching against the pavement. "We found half of a cinnamon roll in Tom's car," he said. "Any chance you can tell me where it came from?"

Lena visibly stiffened, her lips pressing together.

Wilma's stomach sank.

"The cinnamon rolls were mine," Lena said finally, her voice barely above a whisper. "I baked them this morning."

Jason's eyes darkened. "Did Tom buy one?"

Lena shook her head quickly. "Not that I saw. He wasn't even at the bake sale."

Wilma inhaled sharply. "Then... how did he end up with one?"

For a moment, no one spoke. The only sound was the distant chatter of the townsfolk, murmuring amongst themselves.

Jason sighed, rubbing his temple. "We'll need to test everything. For now, I need a list of every single person who bought something from this stall."

Lena swallowed hard. "Of course."

Wilma wasn't looking at her anymore. Her mind had jumped to a different conclusion, one that left a sick feeling in her gut.

She had been given something from the bake sale, too.

Her hand slowly reached into her Easter basket, fingers closing around the foil-wrapped chocolate egg Lena had given her earlier.

She turned it over, her breath catching.

What if the poisoned food wasn't meant for Tom?

What if it was meant for her?

CHAPTER THREE

WILMA'S FINGERS curled around the foil-wrapped chocolate egg in her Easter basket, her heartbeat a slow, steady drumbeat in her ears. The moment she picked it up, a terrible realization settled in her stomach like a stone.

Lena had given it to her.

A special treat, she'd said.

Had it been meant to kill her?

Jason must have caught the change in her expression because he frowned. "Wilma?" His voice had dropped to a quieter, more serious tone.

She held up the chocolate between them. "Lena gave me this before the parade. Said it was a thank-you for keeping the Easter tradition alive."

Jason's eyes sharpened as he took it from her, turning it over in his hands. "Did you eat any of it?"

"No," Wilma said, exhaling. "I was too busy sweating in that awful rabbit suit."

Jason let out a sharp breath. "We need to have this tested with the rest of the pastries." He motioned to one of his deputies, who hurried over with an evidence bag. Carefully, he dropped the foil-wrapped egg inside before sealing it.

Wilma watched it disappear into the deputy's hands, a dizzying sense of unease creeping over her.

"I don't understand," she admitted, shaking her head. "Why would Lena give me something poisoned?"

Jason studied her for a long moment, his expression unreadable. "Do you think she meant to?"

Wilma hesitated. She had spent years reading people—students, parents, strangers, liars—but when Lena had looked at Tom's body in pure horror, Wilma hadn't sensed guilt.

"No," she admitted. "She seemed genuinely shocked."

Jason rubbed his jaw. "Then that means we have two possibilities. Either Lena poisoned multiple people intentionally, or someone else used her baked goods to do it."

Wilma nodded. "And if Tom wasn't the intended victim..."

Jason finished the thought for her. "Then we need to find out who was."

The thought sent an icy chill through Wilma's veins.

If someone had poisoned the baked goods at the sale, then anyone could have been a target.

Including her.

––––––––

Wilma and Jason made their way back to the bake sale tent, where Lena Morgan stood behind the table, arms folded tightly across her chest. The other volunteers had backed away, exchanging anxious whispers as the weight of the situation settled over them.

Lena's face was pale, drawn, her usually bright eyes dark with fear. When she spotted Wilma and Jason approaching, she straightened, her hands gripping the edge of the table as if bracing herself.

"I didn't do anything," she said before either of them could speak. "You have to believe me."

Jason's voice remained even. "Lena, we just need to ask a few questions."

Lena's hands curled into fists, then relaxed just as quickly. "I've been making those cinnamon rolls for years. They're one of my best sellers. There's no way—I mean, it's not possible—" She shook her head, her breath catching. "You really think I poisoned Tom?"

Wilma watched her carefully. If Lena had done this, she was either an exceptional liar or truly panicked at the accusation.

"I saw you hand Wilma a chocolate egg before the parade," Jason said. "Was that from the same batch as the ones you sold?"

Lena blinked at him. "Yes, of course. I made a small batch of special treats to hand out to a few people. Just friends. People I wanted to thank." She looked at Wilma. "You didn't eat it?"

"No," Wilma said. "But Tom ate one of your cinnamon rolls."

Lena's mouth parted slightly. "But he never even came to the bake sale. How did he get one?"

"That's what we're trying to figure out," Jason said. "Are you sure no one else handled the cinnamon rolls?"

Lena hesitated.

"What is it?" Wilma asked.

Lena exhaled, rubbing her hands down the front of her flour-streaked apron. "I set everything up myself, but... Irene Holloway helped with the last-minute packaging. She was putting the pastries into the little paper bags. We were rushing because the line was getting long."

Wilma's mind clicked into motion. If Irene had handled the pastries before they were sold... could someone have slipped something into one of them?

"Where's Irene now?" Jason asked.

Lena turned, scanning the thinning crowd. "She was just here..."

Wilma followed Lena's gaze, but Irene was nowhere to be seen.

The once-busy bake sale tent now felt like something else entirely—a crime scene.

Wilma wasn't sure who had poisoned Tom Alden, but one thing was clear.

Someone had gone through a lot of trouble to make sure the deadly treat landed in the wrong hands.

———

Wilma tightened her coat against the chill in the air as she approached Alden's Auto, the town's main car maintenance and used vehicle sales shop. The garage sat just on the edge of Barwick's downtown, a large red-brick building with two open bays, the scent of motor oil and tire rubber lingering in the air.

A sign by the entrance read: CLOSED TODAY – IN MEMORY OF TOM ALDEN.

The weight of his death had settled over the town like a dense fog. It wasn't just the shock of losing someone well-liked—it was the way it had happened. Unexpected. Public. Suspicious.

Wilma pushed open the side door, stepping into the main garage. The place was eerily quiet, the usual hum of activity missing. A few employees stood in a cluster near the back, murmuring in hushed tones.

She spotted Dean Harper, a former mechanic who had left town years ago after a falling out with Tom. Now he was back, arms crossed, expression unreadable as he listened to his coworkers.

Dean had never been particularly warm toward Wilma. He was rough around the edges, the kind of man who spoke in short, clipped sentences and never had time for small talk. When he noticed her standing by the door, his brows lifted slightly.

"What are you doing here, Miss Wade?" His voice carried a hint of impatience.

Wilma met his gaze evenly. "Just checking in."

Dean scoffed. "Checking in? Or looking for something?"

Wilma ignored the jab. "Tom was a friend. I just wanted to see how everyone's holding up."

A few of the younger mechanics looked away, their grief too raw to put into words.

Dean exhaled sharply and rubbed the back of his neck. "It's a damn mess, that's what it is."

Wilma stepped further inside, keeping her voice gentle. "I heard you and Tom had a disagreement years ago."

Dean's eyes flashed. "That was a long time ago."

"And yet, you're back now," Wilma said, watching his reaction carefully. "You were at the parade, weren't you?"

Dean's jaw tightened. "So were a lot of people."

"True," Wilma conceded. "But not everyone had a history with Tom."

Dean's hands curled into fists, but he didn't speak. The tension between them stretched long and thin, like an old wire that might snap at any second.

Finally, he let out a low breath and shook his head. "I came back because Tom and I were talking about making things right. He was thinking about selling part of the business. Letting me buy in."

Wilma blinked. That was new information. "He never mentioned that to me."

Dean shrugged. "Guess he didn't get the chance."

A chill ran down Wilma's spine. Tom had been planning something big, something that could have affected a lot of people. And now, just like that, he was gone.

She took a step closer. "Dean, did Tom seem worried about anything?"

Dean hesitated. "I don't know. Maybe. He was acting a little off lately."

"How so?"

Dean frowned. "Just… checking over his shoulder more. Said he'd made some bad financial decisions a while back and was trying to fix them. But he didn't get into details."

Wilma's breath caught. Bad financial decisions. Could that have been the real reason Tom was killed?

She turned toward the open bay doors, staring out at the quiet street beyond, her mind already fitting the puzzle pieces together.

Tom Alden hadn't been poisoned by accident.

Someone had wanted him dead.

CHAPTER FOUR

WILMA STEPPED into Tom Alden's office, the scent of motor oil, old paper, and coffee lingering in the air. The space was small, cluttered but not messy, the kind of place where a man spent more time working than organizing. A battered wooden desk stood in the center, its surface covered in invoices, receipts, and handwritten notes.

Wilma ran her fingers along the desk's edge, her mind turning over everything she had learned so far. Poisoned food. Financial problems. A half-finished business deal. If she wanted to understand why Tom was killed, she needed to start with what he had been trying to fix before he died.

She pulled out the top drawer, flipping through a stack of business invoices. Most were for car repairs, sales transactions, and equipment orders, but one folder stuck out—marked with a red tab, unlike the others.

She set it on the desk and flipped it open.

Inside were ledgers filled with numbers that made her frown. Some of the amounts looked too large, others too frequent, as if

Tom had been making withdrawals for something beyond his usual expenses.

Her fingers traced a handwritten list on the last page. Three names stood out.

Dean Harper. Lena Morgan. Irene Holloway.

Wilma's pulse quickened.

Dean had just told her that Tom was considering selling part of the business. But why was Lena's name here? She had nothing to do with the garage. And Irene—the woman who had helped package the baked goods at the parade—what connection could she possibly have to Tom's finances?

Before she could dig further, a noise outside the door made her freeze.

A slow, deliberate shuffle of footsteps.

Someone was standing just outside the office, waiting.

Wilma's breath caught as she quickly closed the folder, her mind racing. Whoever was out there—they didn't want her snooping around.

———

Wilma straightened, her pulse quickening as the footsteps stopped just outside the office door. She kept her hand over the folder of financial records, pressing it flat against the desk as if she could hide it by sheer will alone.

The door creaked open.

A tall, broad-shouldered man filled the doorway. Rick Thompson.

Wilma recognized him immediately—the owner of Thompson Auto, the only other garage in Barwick. He had always been territorial about business, but she'd never known him to be outright hostile. Now, his gaze swept the office with a look of suspicion, landing on Wilma.

"What are you doing in here?" Rick's voice was flat, but there was an edge beneath it.

Wilma kept her posture relaxed. "Just paying my respects. Looking for answers."

Rick stepped further inside, the door clicking shut behind him. "You think you'll find them in Tom's desk?"

Wilma didn't blink. "I think Tom was in trouble before he died."

Rick exhaled sharply, shaking his head. "You don't know what you're talking about."

"I know Tom owed someone money," Wilma said evenly. "And I know his business was struggling more than most people realized."

Rick's mouth pressed into a thin line. "Yeah. Because he made stupid decisions. He thought he could handle things on his own. Guess it caught up with him."

Wilma studied him carefully. Angry, but not defensive. His fists were clenched, but his face didn't have the tension of a man trying to cover up a crime—he looked frustrated, not guilty.

"You had a deal with him, didn't you?" Wilma pressed. "Something he was trying to back out of?"

Rick exhaled, running a hand through his graying hair. "Yeah. He was gonna sell me part of the shop, let me absorb some of his customer base. Then, at the last minute, he changed his mind. Said he needed more time. He was scrambling, Wade. Trying to fix something big."

Wilma's fingers curled slightly against the desk. "And that made you angry."

Rick let out a short, humorless laugh. "Of course it made me angry. You think I killed him over a bad business deal?" He stepped closer, his presence looming. "If I wanted Tom gone, I'd have fought him fair and square. I don't do cowardly crap like poisoning."

Wilma held his gaze. She believed him. Rick was many things, but a man who worked with his hands and his fists wasn't likely to resort to something as calculated as poison.

Before either of them could say more, the door swung open again.

Jason Fellow stepped inside, his badge already out, his eyes flicking between Rick's stiff stance and Wilma's unreadable expression.

"This a bad time?" Jason asked, his tone casual but firm.

Rick let out a breath. "I was just leaving."

Jason didn't move until Rick brushed past him, pushing open the door a little harder than necessary as he left.

Once they were alone, Jason turned back to Wilma. "What did he say?"

Wilma let out a slow breath. "That Tom backed out of selling him part of the garage."

Jason frowned. "So, he was holding onto something. Something worth fighting for."

Wilma nodded. "And maybe something worth killing for."

———

Jason closed the office door, his gaze shifting to the folder on Tom's desk. Wilma watched as his brow furrowed, recognizing the weight of what they had just uncovered.

"This isn't just about a failing business," Jason said, stepping closer. "Tom was holding onto something. Maybe even trying to fix a mistake before it caught up to him."

Wilma tapped the folder. "And I think these numbers might tell us what that mistake was."

Jason pulled on a pair of gloves and opened the ledger, flipping through the pages filled with erratic transactions. Wilma leaned over, pointing at a series of large withdrawals over the past six months.

"These aren't normal expenses," she said. "And look at the timing—these amounts kept getting bigger."

Jason's lips pressed into a thin line. "Someone was squeezing him."

Wilma nodded. "And the names at the back of the ledger—Dean Harper, Lena Morgan, Irene Holloway. What do they have in common?"

Jason turned to the last page, scanning the names. "Dean was a mechanic here, but Lena and Irene? The only connection they have is the bake sale."

Wilma felt her stomach tighten. "Exactly. If someone tampered with the food, we're looking at one of two things—either Tom was never the intended target, or someone used the bake sale as a cover."

Jason exhaled sharply. "If Lena's name is in here, she might have known something. Maybe Tom owed her money. Maybe she knew who he was paying."

Wilma frowned. "But if she had a reason to poison him, why would she give me a chocolate egg? That doesn't fit."

Jason leaned back against the desk, arms crossed. "That's what we need to figure out. Either Lena's involved, or someone's setting her up."

Wilma's thoughts raced. "And Irene—she handled the pastries. If someone slipped something into the food, she could've seen it."

Jason nodded. "Which means she's our next stop."

Wilma grabbed her coat. "Let's go."

As they left the office, Wilma couldn't shake the feeling that they were running out of time—and that whoever had planned Tom's death wasn't done yet.

CHAPTER FIVE

THE HOLLOWAY HOUSE sat at the very edge of Barwick, a small, weathered home with flower pots lining the front steps and a white rocking chair swaying slightly in the afternoon breeze. Wilma had always known Irene Holloway to be a quiet, unassuming woman, someone who kept to herself but never caused trouble. Today, however, something about the house felt... different.

Jason knocked firmly on the front door. The sound echoed, but no response came.

Wilma glanced at him. "She's home. Look—the curtain just moved."

Jason sighed and knocked again, louder this time. "Irene? It's Jason Fellow. We need to talk."

A long pause. Then, slowly, the door creaked open.

Irene Holloway stood just inside the doorway, her small frame hunched slightly, her face pale. She wasn't wearing her usual friendly expression—she looked troubled, wary, as if she had already guessed why they were here.

"I... I don't know what I can tell you," Irene said hesitantly, clutching the doorframe. "I already spoke to one of your deputies at the parade."

Wilma gave her a measured look. "We're not here about the parade itself, Irene. We're here about the bake sale."

Irene swallowed. "I told them everything I know."

Wilma tilted her head slightly, watching the way Irene's fingers twitched against the wooden door. A small lie, just barely detectable.

Jason's voice remained calm, but firm. "You were handling the baked goods before they were sold, weren't you?"

"Yes," Irene said quickly. Too quickly.

"And you never saw anything unusual? No one handling the pastries besides you and Lena?"

A hesitation. Barely a flicker, but Wilma caught it.

"No," Irene said.

Wilma stepped forward slightly, softening her voice. "Irene, I know this is scary. But Tom Alden was poisoned, and we think it might have happened through the baked goods. If there's anything—anything at all—that you remember, we need to know."

Irene's hands gripped the edge of the doorframe tighter. "I... I don't know..."

Jason exhaled sharply, rubbing the bridge of his nose. "Irene, if you know something and you're not telling us, it could put someone else in danger."

That did it.

Irene's face crumpled slightly, her eyes darting around as if checking for listening ears. She took a slow breath, then stepped back, opening the door wider.

"Come in," she whispered.

Jason shot Wilma a quick glance before they both stepped inside.

The living room smelled faintly of cinnamon and old books, a knitted throw draped over the arm of a well-loved chair. Irene motioned them to sit, but remained standing herself, wringing her hands together as if debating whether to speak.

Finally, she took a breath.

"I... I did see something."

Wilma and Jason leaned in.

Irene licked her lips, her voice dropping lower. "Right before the parade started, I saw someone near the baked goods. They weren't supposed to be there."

Jason's expression darkened. "Who?"

Irene hesitated, shifting from foot to foot.

Then she finally whispered:

"Rick Thompson."

———

Jason's expression hardened at the name, but Wilma wasn't convinced.

"Rick Thompson?" Jason repeated, his voice skeptical. "Are you sure?"

Irene nodded, though her hands were still twisting anxiously at the hem of her cardigan. "I saw him near the tables just before the parade started. He wasn't buying anything. He looked... nervous. Rushed. Like he was trying to get in and out without being noticed."

Wilma studied her closely. "Did he touch anything?"

Irene's eyes darted to the side, and for a moment, Wilma thought she was going to change her story. But then Irene sighed. "I —I don't know. I was busy putting everything into the little paper bags. I just remember looking up and seeing him there, just for a second."

Jason crossed his arms. "Rick told me earlier that he was furious at Tom for backing out of their business deal. Maybe he was desperate enough to do something about it."

Wilma wasn't sure.

Rick had been angry, yes. And clearly frustrated about Tom's sudden change of heart. But poisoning? That seemed too calculated for a man like him. Rick was blunt, the kind of man who solved his problems with his fists, not a vial of poison.

Still, Wilma had to consider the possibility.

She turned back to Irene. "Why didn't you mention this earlier?"

Irene flinched slightly. "I—I wasn't sure it mattered. And honestly, I was scared."

Jason leaned forward slightly. "Why would you be scared, Irene?"

She hesitated. "Because... if he did do something, and he finds out I told you, I don't want to be next."

The words hung heavy in the air.

Jason exhaled through his nose, his jaw tightening. "Alright. We'll talk to him. And leave your name out of it."

Irene gave him a small, relieved nod, but Wilma wasn't done yet.

One more question was bothering her.

"You helped Lena package the cinnamon rolls," Wilma said carefully. "Did you see who bought the one that ended up in Tom's car?"

Irene's fingers gripped the hem of her cardigan even tighter. "No," she said, shaking her head. "But I remember that batch—we were rushing, trying to get everything bagged up in time. I must have packed over a dozen of them."

Wilma frowned. That meant the poisoned cinnamon roll could have landed in anyone's hands.

Which brought her back to the same unsettling question.

Was Tom even the intended victim?

Or had the poison been meant for someone else?

For her?

Wilma and Jason left Irene's house, stepping onto the quiet street. The air felt thicker now, heavier with the weight of uncertainty. Irene's story had only deepened the mystery.

Jason exhaled sharply as they walked toward his car. "Rick Thompson at the bake sale? Doesn't sit right with me."

Wilma agreed. "Rick isn't exactly a subtle man. If he wanted Tom gone, he'd have handled it in a more direct way."

Jason nodded. "Poisoning a cinnamon roll doesn't fit his style."

Wilma thought back to their confrontation with Rick at Tom's garage. He had been frustrated, angry about the business deal falling through, but not the type to resort to something as calculated as this. And yet, Irene had seen him near the food.

"Irene could be lying," Jason said, starting the car.

Wilma glanced at him. "Or she could be telling the truth—but about the wrong person."

Jason gave her a sharp look. "You think she's protecting someone?"

Wilma's hands rested on her lap, her fingers absently twisting her coat button. "Maybe. Or maybe she just doesn't realize what she actually saw."

Jason's expression darkened. "We need to talk to Rick again."

Wilma was about to respond when Jason suddenly hit the brakes, his eyes locking on something ahead.

Wilma's heart jumped.

Her cottage door was slightly ajar.

A cold wave of dread washed over her.

Jason was already out of the car, his hand resting on his holster as he moved toward the front door.

Wilma followed, her breath catching in her throat. She had locked the door before leaving—she was certain of it.

Jason pushed the door open fully, stepping inside first. Wilma followed cautiously.

The living room looked untouched, but the air inside felt... wrong.

Jason moved toward the kitchen, and that's where they saw it.

The drawer where Wilma kept her mail was open, papers scattered across the counter. The cabinet doors were slightly ajar, as if someone had searched through them in a hurry.

Wilma's pulse quickened. "Someone was looking for something."

Jason's jaw tightened. "Or sending a message."

Wilma swallowed hard. "Whoever poisoned Tom... they're not done yet."

CHAPTER SIX

WILMA CROSSED her arms as Jason moved through her cottage, checking for any signs of forced entry. She could tell from his tight jaw and focused expression that he wasn't treating this lightly.

But nothing had been stolen. No cash, no jewelry, not even the small stash of emergency money she kept in the kitchen drawer.

Whoever had broken in wasn't looking for valuables.

Jason crouched near the front door, running a hand along the frame. "No forced entry," he muttered. "Either you forgot to lock up—"

"I didn't," Wilma interrupted firmly.

Jason met her gaze, then nodded. "Then someone had a key."

Wilma's stomach turned. "Or they picked the lock. Either way, they wanted to get in and out without drawing attention."

Jason stood and surveyed the mess in the kitchen—scattered papers, open drawers, nothing missing but everything disturbed.

Wilma's eyes landed on her Easter basket, still sitting on the small table near the door. She frowned and stepped toward it. The basket was overturned, the contents scattered everywhere.

Her breath caught.

Jason noticed her expression change. "What is it?"

Wilma pointed at the overturned basket. "Someone searched my basket."

Jason's expression darkened. "Why would someone do that?"

"Nothing is missing. They must have been looking for the chocolate egg, the one that I gave you," Wilma said slowly. "They weren't looking for money, Jason. They were looking for evidence."

Jason cursed under his breath. "Then they know we suspect the poison might have been meant for you."

Wilma exhaled sharply, her mind racing. The break-in wasn't random. It was a sign that whoever was behind Tom Alden's death was watching her.

Jason turned to her, his expression unreadable. "This isn't just about solving a mystery anymore, Wilma. Someone sees you as a threat."

Wilma refused to let fear take hold. "Then that means I'm close."

Jason sighed, rubbing a hand over his face. "Yeah. And that also means they might try again."

Wilma squared her shoulders. "Let them try."

Jason let out a frustrated huff, clearly unimpressed with her bravado. "I'm not joking, Wilma. I need you to take this seriously."

"I am," she said, voice steady. "But I've lived in this town for decades. I know its people, and I know when someone is trying to scare me off."

Jason shook his head. "And it's working."

Wilma tilted her chin. "Not in the way they want it to."

Jason muttered something under his breath, then crossed the room and locked her front door himself. "Fine. But until we figure out who's behind this, I want someone checking on you regularly."

Wilma smirked. "Worried about me, Jason?"

Jason gave her a long, exasperated look. "You're impossible."

Wilma simply smiled, but inside, she was already turning over the pieces of the puzzle, determined to fit them together.

Whoever had broken into her home had made one critical mistake.

They'd shown her just how desperate they were to keep their secret buried.

———

Jason's phone buzzed as they stood in Wilma's kitchen, still surveying the mess left behind by the intruder. He pulled it from his pocket and answered with a clipped, "Fellow."

Wilma watched as his expression darkened.

"You sure?" Jason asked, pacing a short line near the counter. "Alright. Stay on him, but don't make a move yet."

He ended the call and turned to Wilma, his jaw tight. "That was Deputy Reed. Rick Thompson says he wasn't anywhere near the bake sale."

Wilma frowned. "That doesn't match what Irene told us."

"Exactly," Jason said. "Rick claims he was at his shop the entire morning, getting paperwork in order for a deal he was negotiating. He swears up and down he never even walked through the parade grounds."

Wilma's thoughts churned. "So, either Rick is lying, or Irene is."

Jason sat heavily in one of the chairs, rubbing his chin. "Rick isn't exactly a trustworthy guy, but poisoning someone at a public event? It doesn't fit his usual playbook."

Wilma agreed. "If anything, I'd say Rick was the kind of man who'd settle his grievances face-to-face. This?" She gestured toward the mess around them. "This is sneaky. Calculated."

Jason nodded. "Which means either someone's framing Rick, or Irene is covering for someone."

Wilma sat across from him, her fingers drumming lightly

against the tabletop. "What if Irene didn't actually see Rick at the bake sale? What if she saw someone else and just assumed it was him?"

Jason leaned forward. "You think she misidentified the person?"

"She was distracted," Wilma pointed out. "Rushing to pack pastries, moving around, handling money. If she only caught a glimpse of someone near the baked goods, she might have assumed it was Rick because she already had reason to be wary of him."

Jason sighed. "That's possible. But what if she wasn't mistaken? What if she's covering for someone she's afraid of?"

Wilma nodded slowly. "We still don't know why Irene's name was in Tom's ledger."

Jason tapped the table. "Which means we need to start looking into Irene's financial situation. If Tom was paying her—or if she owed him money—that's a lead we need to follow."

Wilma's thoughts raced. There was something missing, something just beyond her grasp. If Irene had a reason to lie, that meant she had a reason to be afraid.

And that meant they weren't just chasing a killer—they were chasing someone with a lot to lose.

Jason's phone buzzed again. He read the message, his eyes narrowing.

"What is it?" Wilma asked.

Jason stood, grabbing his coat. "It's time we had another talk with Irene Holloway."

———

The ride to Irene Holloway's house was tense. Wilma sat in the passenger seat, hands clasped in her lap, her mind spinning with the possibilities. If Irene was covering for someone, who could it be? And more importantly, why?

Jason pulled up to the modest house and parked, his jaw tight.

He didn't move right away, gripping the steering wheel as he thought through their next steps.

"She's either going to double down on her story," he said finally, "or she's going to crack."

Wilma glanced at the dimly lit porch. "Let's hope it's the latter."

They stepped out of the car and approached the front door. Jason knocked firmly. Nothing.

He knocked again, louder this time. Still no answer.

Wilma's stomach twisted. "She was home earlier."

Jason tried the doorknob. It turned easily—the door wasn't locked.

Wilma's heart started pounding.

Jason glanced at her. "Stay behind me."

Wilma ignored him and stepped in right behind him as he pushed the door open.

The inside of the house was silent. Too silent.

Wilma's eyes adjusted to the dim light filtering through the curtains. The air smelled faintly of coffee and something floral, but underneath that, there was something off.

A chair in the living room was tipped over. A half-empty cup of tea sat on the side table, abandoned.

Jason's body tensed. "Irene?" His voice echoed in the house.

No response.

They moved deeper inside. Wilma's pulse quickened with every step.

And then she saw it.

A piece of paper, hastily torn from a notebook, lay on the kitchen counter. Wilma stepped closer, Jason right behind her.

The note was written in shaky handwriting.

I didn't mean to get involved. I didn't know. Please, don't let them find me.

Wilma's breath caught. "Jason…"

He was already moving, his phone in hand. "We need units here now. Irene Holloway is missing."

Wilma swallowed hard, rereading the note. Not a confession. Not an explanation. A plea.

Whoever had killed Tom Alden... was still out there.

And now, Irene was gone.

CHAPTER SEVEN

AS JASON DROVE OFF, Wilma rubbed her hands over her eyes. Everything seemed so confusing. Who had killed Tom? Was it related to Irene's disappearance?

She decided to poke around the house some more. Maybe Irene had left other clues. As she looked around the house, she noticed that there were several pictures on the walls showing a similar vantage point.

Wilma studied the pictures, hoping to find some landmark she could use to guide Jason to where Irene was.

Footsteps sounded behind her and she turned. A gasp ripped from her throat as she stared down the barrel of a gun.

"You're not Irene!" a furious voice said.

Wilma looked down the length of the gun to the man holding it. "Dean Harper?"

Dean's jaw clenched. "Where's Irene?"

"I don't know." Wilma slowly lifted her hands. "What are you doing with the gun, Dean?"

Dean didn't answer. His eyes were wild and frightened. He

lunged at her suddenly and grabbed her arm. Wilma twisted her arm away from him but Dean pointed the gun at her again.

"Don't fight or I'll shoot you," he warned.

Wilma swallowed. "What are you going to do?"

He dragged her toward the door. "I don't have anything against you, Miss Wade. In fact, I think you're a nice old lady. But I can't let you go, not now. Come on."

He dragged her outside and with the barrel of the gun in her ribs, made her get into his car.

"Drive to the old dam," he said, his hands tight on the gun. "There's an old basement there... nice and isolated." He nodded to himself, his eyes still wild. "Once I'm away from Barwick, I'll tell them where to find you."

"My body, you mean?" Wilma asked.

Dean winced. "No. No. I'm not going to kill you. I don't want to kill you."

But Wilma heard in his voice that he didn't really mean it. She could identify him. She fought to remain calm. "Did you kill Tom?"

"Don't ask me that," Dean pleaded.

Wilma tried to stay calm. "You did, didn't you? You found the pastry that was labeled for him and poisoned it. Was it because of business?"

"Business," Dean repeated. "No. It's not because of business. It's because he ruined my life! But Lena, she saw everything. She saw me poison the pastry. I thought she was going to tell Fellow everything, but she tried to blackmail me instead."

"So you came to her house to kill her," Wilma realized. "Only you found me instead."

They were out of town now. Wilma's mind raced as she tried to think of how to get out of this. If they reached the dam, she was sure Dean would kill her. But if she didn't keep driving, he would shoot her here.

"I can help you with the police," she said.

"I'm not turning myself in," Dean snapped. His grip tightened on his gun.

Wilma swallowed hard. "But I can help you frame Lena for it. Who will believe her testimony if it looks like she's the killer?"

Dean grew uncertain. He was thinking about her offer. Wilma hoped he would take it. But then her hopes were dashed as he shook his head.

"No, it's too risky. How can I trust you?" he said.

The dam was only ten minutes away now. Wilma's life flashed before her eyes. She had wanted to leave a mark on the world, had wanted to accomplish more than what she had done.

If I get out of this, I'm going to publish one of my books. I'll stop hiding, she vowed.

What about her cousin Martha? She had just lost her husband, she would be so distraught to lose Wilma, too. And Jason would blame himself, she was sure. She thought of all her friends in Barwick and with an aching heart, realized that she was leaving behind more than she realized.

The only comfort she could muster up was that her beloved fiancé who had died decades ago would be waiting for her.

If I'm going to die, I'm at least going to have answers, she decided.

"Was the pastry the only thing that you poisoned? I was given a poisoned chocolate egg. Were you behind that, too?" Wilma asked.

Dean's eyes grew large. "No! I have no reason to want you to die."

"Then who does?" she wondered out loud. "And if Lena was blackmailing you, why is she missing now?"

"Lena's missing?" Dean asked.

Wilma pulled the car to a stop at the old dam. She tightened her grip on the steering wheel and turned to Dean. "I know that you're afraid, Dean. But really, killing me is only going to make things more difficult for you. Don't make this worse for yourself."

Dean lifted his gun. "I'm sorry, Miss Wade. But I don't have a choice. Get out."

"Dean, please."

He cocked the gun and aimed it at her. Wilma reluctantly got out of the car.

"We'll go to the top of the dam," Dean muttered. He wasn't trying to convince himself not to kill her anymore. "Yes. The top of the dam. March."

Wilma headed for the rusty ladder on the side of the dam. Just as she started to climb, though, a dozen police cars showed up.

"Hands up, Dean!" Jason yelled, pointing his gun at Dean.

Dean's eyes widened. He put his hands in the air as his shoulders slumped.

Wilma hurried away from him. Jason rushed to her side and checked if she was okay.

"I am. Dean killed Tom. He told me. How did you find me?" Wilma asked.

Jason put an arm around her shoulder. "I saw you driving off with him and knew something was wrong. Come on. Let's get you home. I bet you could use a cup of tea."

Wilma laughed, shaken but grateful. "Yes, please. A cup of tea will be very nice."

EPILOGUE

WILMA SAT at her kitchen table, flipping through the morning edition of the *Barwick Gazette*. The front page bore the headline:

MURDER AT THE PARADE—LOCAL BUSINESS OWNER POISONED, KILLER ARRESTED

She skimmed the article, her fingers tightening around her mug of tea as she read. It laid out the official version of events—the poisoned cinnamon roll at the bake sale, the financial disputes surrounding Tom Alden, and the arrest of the culprit.

According to the paper, it was a clean case.

Too clean.

Wilma sighed, setting the paper down. Jason had closed the investigation, and Irene Holloway was found alive after her disappearance. But the way she had begged them not to let 'them' find her—that haunted Wilma.

Because who was 'them'?

She traced the rim of her teacup with her finger, thinking about the break-in at her cottage, the poisoned chocolate egg, the lingering fear in Irene's voice. There were too many unanswered questions, and if there was one thing Wilma couldn't stand, it was an unfinished story.

A knock at the door pulled her from her thoughts.

Jason stood on her porch, holding two coffee cups, his badge glinting slightly under the morning sun.

She opened the door and waved him in. "You bringing peace offerings now?"

Jason smirked, handing her a cup. "Figured you'd need something stronger than tea."

Wilma took the coffee but didn't sip it right away. "You're here because you still don't think this case is wrapped up either, aren't you?"

Jason exhaled sharply, setting his own coffee down on the counter. "Irene finally agreed to cooperate. She confirmed she was threatened—warned to keep her mouth shut—but she swears she doesn't know who was behind it."

Wilma folded her arms. "Which means someone else was pulling the strings."

Jason nodded. "We got the person responsible for poisoning Tom, but we didn't get the person who made sure Irene was too scared to talk. I can't help but think she was involved in the attempt to poison you, but she keeps claiming she didn't know the egg was poisoned."

Wilma tilted her head, considering. "And now she's safe?"

Jason's jaw tensed. "For now. But I don't like leaving loose ends. And neither do you."

Wilma let out a short laugh. "You know me too well."

Jason took a sip of his coffee. "I also know you're not going to stop looking into this."

She gave him an innocent shrug. "Wouldn't dream of it."

Jason sighed, rubbing his temple. "Just be careful, Wilma. Someone already broke into your house looking for something. I don't want to be finding you at the bottom of another mystery—literally."

Wilma smiled. "Then let's hope whoever is out there doesn't underestimate me."

Jason huffed, shaking his head, but he didn't argue. Instead, he reached into his pocket and pulled out a small theater flyer, sliding it across the table.

She glanced down. It was for a play at the Barwick Playhouse.

"Why are you handing me this?" she asked, raising an eyebrow.

"Because Irene mentioned something before she went into protective custody. She said she was supposed to meet someone connected to Tom's business—but she was too afraid to go. The meeting was supposed to take place at the playhouse."

Wilma's lips pressed together. "That's an odd place to meet about finances."

Jason nodded. "Which is exactly why it caught my attention."

Wilma traced the edges of the flyer, and something stirring deep in her gut—that familiar pull toward unfinished business.

"Tell me, Jason," she said lightly, "do you like the theater?"

Jason groaned, already regretting bringing it up.

Wilma took a satisfied sip of her coffee.

Maybe this mystery wasn't quite finished after all.

The End

MURDER AT THE PLAYHOUSE

A SMALL-TOWN SPRING COZY MYSTERY WITH A SENIOR SLEUTH

CHAPTER ONE

WILMA WADE HAD, in her younger years, once volunteered to run a production of *Hamlet* at the high school where she taught. The experience had left her swearing never to have anything to do with the theatre ever again. And she had stuck to it for forty-odd years. Perhaps it was the passing of four decades that had dulled her memory of the pain.

Now, backstage at the Barwick High School Theatre, working not with students but volunteers with ages ranging from fifteen to eighty-five, Wilma Wade remembered why she hated the theatre so much.

"How do I keep letting myself get roped into these things?" she grumbled as she glued small tissue leaves to a tree under which the lovers of the play would share their first kiss at the end of Act One. "I could be at home working on my book, but instead I'm here with glue all over my fingers!"

She glanced around guiltily, hoping nobody heard her complaining. If she was honest, the rush of the last-minute stage preparations was actually a bit exhilarating. After the series of murders that had left this seventy-year-old retiree looking under every rock for another mystery, the straightforward direction 'glue leaves to these branches' was a nice change of pace.

It was the annual Spring Festival in Barwick, taking place on the May long weekend, and Wilma had been roped into volunteering with this year's musical performance. It was some sort of musical theatre play thing—Wilma wasn't entirely certain what the proper terminology was. Apparently, it was a well-beloved tradition in Barwick. Wilma had seen posters in years past, but hadn't gone to see a performance herself.

After the last murder that took place in Barwick, when Wilma's life was threatened, she was determined to be more impactful in her community. She'd spent much of her life in mourning. Her fiancé had died when they were young, and she'd been mourning him and the life she thought she would have with him. But it was never too late to turn things around. Someone out there had tried to kill her with a poisoned chocolate egg, and that person was still on the loose.

Wilma wasn't going to waste the rest of her life wishing her past could be different. It didn't happen the way she wanted, no, but she was still strong, her body was able, and she would start really living again.

"Do you need more leaves?" Detective Jason Fellow, whom Wilma worked with to solve mysteries, asked from her elbow. He was pinning apples onto the branches.

"I think that's good," Wilma said as she stepped back to admire her work.

Jason had been the one that roped her into volunteering with the theatre in the first place. He, apparently, was a huge fan of the theatre. How he'd ended up as a police officer was a mystery in and of itself. Wilma thought it must be that he decided to go for a more stable career, one the arts just wouldn't provide.

"I wanted to say—" Jason started.

He was cut off by a loud shout from behind them. "And I'm telling you, she's no good!"

Wilma winced. She knew that voice all too well. Their lead actress, Veronica Lane, stood in the center of the stage. Next to her were the stage manager, Julia Tren, and Veronica's understudy, Beth Calloway.

"Veronica, we've discussed this," Julia said, her voice tense as she looked around, embarrassed by the scene. "You and Beth look similar enough for her to pass as a younger version of you. Tonight is the only night when Beth's mother can see the performance. It's just one solo—"

"I don't care." Veronica tossed her hair imperiously. "You signed a contract. I'm volunteering my considerable talents because this seemed like a worthy cause, all the proceeds going to charity. But if you think you're going to replace me with this no-talent half-wit, I won't perform at all. Then who is going to come to your little play?"

Beth took a shuddering breath. "Please, my mother is—"

Veronica looked down her nose at Beth. "It's not my fault that you're a disappointment to your parents."

And with that, Beth burst into tears. She raced down the stage stairs. Someone went after her while the rest of the stagehands pretended to be busy, trying to observe without being accused of being nosy. Detective Fellow frowned as he strode forward toward where Julia and Veronica's argument was getting louder.

Wilma, generally, found that it was best to keep out of other people's arguments. Rather than defusing situations, she always had the feeling that she was just delaying an even worse fight. But she had also never witnessed such an acidic attitude like the one Veronica was displaying. She shook her head as she followed Jason, so she could lend him her support, too.

"Let's take a step back," Jason said, using his professional Detective voice. "Looks like things are getting heated and we need to cool down, okay?"

"And who are you?" Veronica said, looking down her nose at him the same way she'd looked down on Beth.

Jason didn't budge. "Detective Jason Fellow. And this is Wilma Wade," he added, gesturing to Wilma. "Clearly, there's some tension going on. I suggest we all go our separate ways and come back when we have cooler heads, okay?"

"Or what, you're going to arrest me?" Veronica laughed. She eyed Wilma with disdain. "Oh, I've heard about you. You're that retired teacher who reads her dreadful stories at the hospital. Are you going to give me detention, teacher?"

Wilma felt her ire raise but forced it down. "Julia, why don't you come help me with something?" she said, keeping her voice cool.

Veronica looked annoyed that Wilma didn't rise to her bait. Julia, on the other hand, was grateful for the excuse to leave. Her hands shook as Wilma led her backstage. Once they were well away from Veronica, who was still giving Jason attitude, Wilma asked, "Are you okay?"

Julia nodded, smoothing down her blouse. "I'm fine, thank you. It's just that awful woman. Beth's mother is sick and Veronica is acting as though... well, never mind. If we weren't completely sold out, I would kick her out and put Beth on as our lead. There's way too much buzz about Veronica being our star to change it now."

She ran her fingers through her hair, looking distracted. Then, mumbling excuses, she headed for her office. By that time, Veronica had decided Jason wasn't a very good target and headed backstage, presumably to her dressing room. Wilma returned to the tree, tense from the confrontation. Jason joined her.

"Are you alright?" Jason asked her.

"Fine, fine," Wilma answered.

Jason nodded once. "So have you heard back from that publisher that you sent your novel to?"

Wilma winced. "It was rejected. A very polite rejection, mind you. But it was still a rejection."

She had been trying for some months now, sending her manuscript off to agents and publishers. Everything so far had been a polite rejection. She knew it would take time and normally the rejections didn't bother her. Bringing it up now, after the scene Veronica caused, made Wilma feel extra sensitive about it.

"I'm sorry," Jason said, patting her arm. "These things take time. I loved reading it, I'm sure that sooner or later you'll find someone who will see it for the brilliance that it is."

Wilma smiled gratefully at Jason. She normally thought of herself as a pragmatic sort of person, but this had been quite the test. Even though she knew the chances of being picked up by a publisher right away were negligible, it hadn't stopped her from indulging in the occasional fantasy.

"The problem is, I've put my heart into these stories," Wilma said slowly as she started to gather up the unused leaves for the tree. "And it's like I'm sending my children out to be judged by society. So, when they say it's not good enough, no matter how polite it is, it feels like my best efforts aren't enough."

Veronica's statement about Wilma reading her stories at the hospital didn't help, either. Wilma had to admit, she wondered if she was good enough to share at all.

"The people at the hospital seem to enjoy my short stories. Maybe that's where my talent is. Maybe I'm only good enough for small-town things," she said slowly.

"Don't talk like that," Jason said. He pinned on his last apple and put a bracing hand on her shoulder. "You're clever, passionate, and starting a new venture. Don't you know how many rejections some of our most famous writers had before they were picked up? Just because someone hasn't taken your book yet doesn't mean it's not worth keeping going."

Wilma smiled her gratitude at Jason. It was very strange, starting on such a new path after all these years. She'd thought that she would live a quiet retirement in a quiet town. She had never anticipated that this move would start up new paths for her.

After several hours of frantic work, everything was ready. The theatre was filling up and Wilma was backstage with the actors, making sure they had everything they needed for their performance. She'd baked some cookies for the cast, and laid them out as a snack to bolster energy levels while they worked.

"It's almost time," Julia called, clapping her hands for attention. She looked over the gathered faces and her expression fell to a frown. "Where's Veronica?"

Everyone glanced around. Wilma felt a surge of irritation go through her. It was almost time for the curtains to go up and Veronica was nowhere to be seen. She was certain that someone had knocked on Veronica's dressing room earlier. She glanced at Detective Fellow, lifting her eyebrows. He shook his head.

"I knocked on her door," one of the young interns said. "I opened the door and told her we're supposed to be gathering, but she just ignored me."

"I'll go get her," Wilma volunteered. She might have let Veronica get under her skin earlier in the day, but she didn't want any of these young kids ending up in tears because of Veronica's verbal abuse.

"Thank you, Wilma," Julia said. "In the meantime…"

She gave the cast a pep talk as Wilma headed to the star's dressing room. When she knocked, there was no answer. Wilma sighed, wondering if all of this really was worth it. Was Veronica that good of an actress? Maybe it was just her personal opinion, but Beth was just as good. And much easier to deal with.

But Veronica was famed in Barwick. She'd done a few performances in New York, or so the rumors went. Everyone talked about how excited they were to see her on the home stage again.

There was still no answer so Wilma knocked again. She opened the door. It swung open to reveal Veronica sitting in her chair, her back to the door. The mirror was angled so that Wilma couldn't see her face.

"Veronica, it's time to—" Wilma cut off.

The actress was slumped slightly in her chair, one of her arms dangling toward the floor. A sinking feeling swept through Wilma.

She recognized that color of skin, the rigid yet limp way Veronica was sitting.

Swallowing, Wilma crept into the dressing room. She scanned the area, committing everything to memory and making sure she didn't disturb anything.

Finally, she stepped around the chair to see Veronica's face. Wilma instantly knew she was dead. There was no mistaking it. She put a hand to her chest, shaking her head as sadness swept through her.

Just as she was about to go back to tell Detective Fellow, something caught her eye. Something thin and metal around Veronica's neck. She bent closer and gasped. It was a guitar string.

Vernica Lane wasn't just dead.

She had been murdered.

CHAPTER TWO

DETECTIVE FELLOW CURTAINED off the dressing room. "This is bad business," he said to Wilma after he called it in. "The forensic team will be here shortly. We need to keep everyone calm and away from the room in the meantime. This is terrible for the charity, but we have no choice but to send the audience home."

"What if someone in the audience killed her?" Wilma asked, anxious.

"It won't do any good to keep them here. If it was someone in the audience, my guess is that they wouldn't have stuck around. They probably fled immediately. But judging by the body's state, it looks like she's been dead for a few hours." Jason lowered his voice as he leaned his head toward her. "My guess is that it's someone in the production company."

Wilma nodded. That made sense. "Who do you want to start questioning?"

"I have to stay here and keep an eye on the body. But if you can figure out who was the last person to see her alive, that's a good place to start," Jason said.

"I'll start asking around," Wilma promised, determined not to let him down.

Where to start? Wilma decided to ask the other volunteers that worked on the set designs first. She approached Linden Bridgerton, who had his arms folded tightly across his chest.

"Isn't it just awful business?" Wilma asked.

Lindon nodded. "I can't believe it. Veronica was so talented! So… so larger than life. It seems impossible that she's dead."

"I can't believe it, either," Wilma agreed. "I keep thinking about that big fight she had with Julia. Where did she go afterward?"

"I think she went straight to her dressing room," Lindon said. "I remember hearing a door slam. But then a little while later, I heard another door slam. Maybe it was someone else going into the dressing room? But then I realized that some of the sand bags were leaking and I had to go take care of them. I didn't see anyone."

Henry Maxwell strutted over. He was the leading man, well known and famous for his handsome face. He'd been eavesdropping on the conversation. "Veronica bowed out of the play, did she? Good riddance to bad rubbish! Beth's twice the actress anyway."

Wilma turned to him. "Veronica Lane didn't bow out of the production. She's been murdered."

"What?" Henry's face went white. He slowly sank into a chair. "Murdered?"

"Why would you think that she simply left the production?" Wilma asked, curious. It didn't seem at all likely for Veronica to just up and leave, not with the big stink she had made over Beth not being good enough to replace her as lead actress.

Henry covered his face with his hands. "Murdered! I never would have… oh, how? Who did it?"

"That's what the police are looking into," Wilma said. She studied Henry Maxwell. Was his shock real or was he faking it? His skin had dropped in color when she'd said Veronica was murdered. You could fake a lot of things, but not physical reactions like that, right? "Henry, what do you know about Veronica? Does she have any enemies in her personal life?"

"I..." Henry swallowed hard as his head came up. "It's just too much of a shock. Forgive me. I need a moment before I answer any questions."

He turned away, hiding his face in his hands again.

By this time, Detective Fellow's forensic team had showed up. They started to process the crime scene as Wilma returned to the back room with the rest of the cast. Henry still seemed in a state of shock. Everyone was whispering to each other.

"Do you think Julia did it?" one of the cast members whispered. "I saw her going backstage after that terrible fight."

"Julia wouldn't hurt a fly," someone else said.

Beth folded her arms over her chest. "Listen to all of you! You're all gossiping and speculating as though this is some sort of... of entertainment! A woman is dead. Have none of you any shame?"

Tears glimmered in her eyes. Most people turned away, looking ashamed. Henry gave Beth a strange sort of look, almost like he suspected her. Wilma studied Beth for a moment. She certainly seemed shocked by all of this. She wouldn't stop trembling. But she had also fought with Veronica earlier. Veronica had been quite cruel to her, in fact.

Wilma made up her mind and approached the young actress. "Beth, I'm so sorry to hear about your mother. I know this isn't the best time, but I wanted to let you know that I'm here for you if you need to talk."

Beth gave her a startled look. "My mother?"

"I heard she was very sick."

"Oh. Yes, yes, she is. I don't know how I'm going to tell her that the play is..." Beth shook her head, then lowered her voice. "I know it's none of my business, but you work with Detective Fellow sometimes, right?"

Wilma nodded.

Beth chewed her lip. "I heard her and our musical director,

Andrew, arguing a few times over the last week. I don't know what it was about, but it might be something the police need to know."

"It might be important," Wilma agreed. "And you don't know what they were arguing about at all?"

Beth opened her mouth then closed it again. Her shoulders hunched as she glanced over Wilma's shoulder at Henry. "No," she said, too quickly. "I have no idea. I didn't want to eavesdrop so I walked away. Do you think I can go, Miss Wade? I need to see to my mother. She's going to be so worried about me and... all of this."

Beth looked so frightened and young that Wilma's heart went out to her. She hugged the younger woman, patting her back.

"Of course. I'll let Detective Fellow know where you've gone. If you can think of anything else that might be useful, just call me or the detective, alright?" Wilma said.

"Thank you, Miss Wade," Beth said, sniffing. Tears welled in her eyes. "You really are the nicest person in town, you know that?"

Wilma blushed, embarrassed and pleased with the praise. Beth gathered her things and headed out as Wilma looked around the room, seeking out Andrew. He was a tall, lanky man with beautiful eyes and a soft face. He looked like the sort of man that you could find yourself confiding in when you didn't really know him, he just had that kind vibe to him.

Right now, he was crying quietly into a shredded tissue. Wilma headed over to him and offered him a new tissue.

"Thank you," Andrew said, sniffing. "I just can't believe it. Veronica... she was so vivacious. So full of life. I can't believe that she's d...d...dead."

He burst into tears and buried his face into the tissue again. Wilma patted his shoulder. "I'm so sorry, Andrew. Did you know her well?" *And what were you fighting with Veronica about?*

"We were practically engaged," Andrew said. "We've been together for almost two years. Oh, it's been a secret. Veronica has a certain reputation to maintain, after all, and I didn't fit in with her lifestyle. But that was fine with me. I didn't care much for the glamour..."

Wilma stared at him, surprised. "You and Veronica were together?"

"I just bought a ring for her," Andrew said, sniffing.

"Oh. I'm surprised, because I heard that the two of you had been having some fights lately," Wilma said.

Andrew lifted his head. "Who told you that?"

"I heard it around town," Wilma fibbed.

"Oh. Oh, well, I suppose that's true. It was nothing serious, though, just silly things. I loved her so much. I wish I hadn't picked on such small things..." Andrew's lip trembled. "I put off proposing because of our little fights. I shouldn't have done that."

"What?" Henry had come over to get a bottle of water. "What do you mean, you and Veronica?" His voice was loud, carrying through the room. "She and I were dating!"

Everyone in the room went still, staring at the two men. Andrew's jaw dropped and his eyes widened. Wilma looked from Henry to Andrew, her eyes wide. Veronica was dating both men? Henry did seem to be more Veronica's style, physically at least, but it seemed impossible that she could have gotten away with it.

Was jealousy the reason she'd been murdered?

"You can't have been seeing Veronica," Andrew said. He dropped the soaked tissue, looking Henry up and down, confused. "She would have told me."

"And you expect me to believe that she would date you?" Henry poked Andrew in the chest. "I bet you did this. You were jealous and she rejected you, so you killed her!"

Andrew fell back a step, his eyes widening. "I would never harm her!"

"Hold on, hold on," Wilma said, quickly putting herself between them. "Listen to me, both of you. This has been a hard day. Don't start accusing each other. We don't want to have unwarranted accusations flying around."

Henry opened his mouth, then paused. He turned away and his shoulders slumped. "You're right, Miss Wade. I'm sorry. This is just too much."

He started to cry. Wilma patted his shoulder just as Detective Fellow stepped into the room. He looked world-weary, a heavy frown on his face. He met Wilma's gaze and she knew just by the look on his face this was going to be a mess.

CHAPTER THREE

THAT NIGHT, Wilma Wade and Jason Fellow made a plan to find the killer. They had a great number of suspects, and narrowing it down would be quite the chore. The first step in their attack plan were brownies. Wilma baked several dozen and Jason helped her to decorate them and place them on various ornamental plates, ready for launch.

The next morning, Wilma hurled herself into the investigation by taking one of the plates of brownies to Henry Maxwell.

"I just wanted to apologize for that scene yesterday at the theatre," Wilma said, offering Henry the brownies. "Can I come in?"

Henry peered at her suspiciously but nodded. He led her into the living room. Wilma was surprised at how nicely decorated the place was. Henry didn't strike her as the sort to care about interior design. She wondered if he had hired someone to make his house look this good or if there was someone in his life that had done it. Maybe Veronica, if they really were dating?

"It must be difficult for you, being a lead actor," Wilma said, focusing on Henry again.

"You don't know the half of it," Henry answered passionately. "I've been working my butt off for years. Years! I've been in productions off-off Broadway, you know. But you'd never know it, listening to the town. I've been in more plays than Veronica Lane, but she's the big star and people still seem to think that I only got the job for the Spring Festival because I'm Julia's cousin!"

He shook his head, disgusted and distraught. With a loud sigh, he slumped back into his chair.

"That does sound difficult," Wilma agreed sympathetically. "Especially when you have such an obvious passion for acting."

"Thank you, Miss Wade," Henry said, his hand over his heart. "It's so good to have someone to talk to about these things. Nobody in this town understands except B..." He cleared his throat and coughed. "Except Veronica. She understood, being an actress herself."

This was just the opening Wilma was hoping for. She leaned forward, putting on a concerned but confused frown. "If you don't mind me asking, how did you and Veronica end up together in the first place?"

"Oh, you know how it is. Late nights running lines. Practicing the play, wanting to get things just right. And when we started talking about the struggles of acting, well... we just clicked. We ended up talking about everything and anything. We took long walks in the woods and just... grew to know each other in ways we hadn't known before," he said, his gaze growing distant.

It sounded cliché, like something from a movie. Before Wilma could ask more, though, the doorbell rang. Henry excused himself and Wilma took a closer look around the living room. It was very neat, very orderly. The curtains were lace and there were several lovely doilies on the various surfaces. Funny. Most young people didn't use doilies anymore.

Henry returned with Detective Fellow right behind him.

And so started the second leg of the attack.

"Oh. Miss Wade," Jason said coolly. His jaw tightened and he looped his thumbs into his belt. "I wasn't expecting to see you today."

"I could have said the same thing to you, Detective," Wilma said, drawing herself up. She did her best to sound cool and professional as she narrowed her eyes at Jason. She patted her steel-colored hair and glanced at the brownies. "I was just bringing some goodies to Henry. Seeing how yesterday was such a shock."

"A shock indeed," Detective Fellow agreed.

Yesterday, when Beth mentioned Wilma working with Detective Fellow, they realized that they weren't going to get their suspects to open up to her if everyone knew she was working with the police. So, for the next few days, they were going to be 'at odds' with one another. It was perfect to get their killer to lower their guard.

"Let's be honest with this, shall we, Miss Wade?" Detective Fellow said as he stepped forward, ignoring Henry. "You are meddling in this case, the way you meddle with all of my cases. Keep your nose out of it, Miss Wade. You aren't a member of the police and you have no right to go poking around in police business."

Wilma folded her arms. "It's not meddling to visit a friend."

"Please, please," Henry said, lifting his hands into the air. "Let's not get into this nasty business of arguing. It's a difficult time. Miss Wade, there were some other things I wished to speak to you about, if you wanted to wait in the kitchen?"

He widened his eyes slightly, as though begging her to stay. Wilma nodded her agreement and headed to the kitchen. She listened with her ear against the door as Jason launched into an aggressive line of questioning. Henry gave him nothing, so Wilma turned her attention to the kitchen. Dishes were piled up in the sink and two wine glasses sat next to it. A quick search of the cupboards revealed that Henry kept his medications in the cupboards here. A bottle of Midol caught Wilma's eye and she nodded, satisfied with her search.

When Detective Fellow left, Henry came to the kitchen to find

Wilma with two mugs of steaming lavender tea. She smiled sympathetically at him as she offered him one mug.

"Detective Fellow is a bit of a bulldog, isn't he?" Henry
grumbled.

"On that we agree. Although... well, I hate to agree with him on
anything, but it is rather... unfortunate timing. I mean, learning
that you and Veronica lived together," she added.

Henry's brow creased. "Oh, we didn't live together. We've been
seeing each other, but she never stayed over."

"I see," Wilma murmured.

"If I'm honest... I wasn't at all sure if I was going to propose or
break up," Henry said in a rush. "Our relationship was rocky. She
was the one that kept telling me she wanted a big wedding. But I
didn't exactly... well, I didn't really trust her. I thought she might
be using me for my money. I come from a wealthy family, after all."

Wilma's eyes widened. "Oh? But you still bought a ring?"

Henry grimaced. "I was afraid of what she might do if I broke
up with her. You see... I don't know if I should tell you this."

"You can tell me." Wilma put her hand over his. "Please, Henry.
I want to help you."

He swallowed hard and nodded. "I know for a fact that she was
blackmailing people, not only in the city but here in town, too. She
didn't name names, but she would always get these mysterious
packages of money. And she told me once that if I ever tried to
leave her, she would make me pay. During our time together she...
learned things about me."

"What sort of—" Wilma cut herself off when Henry winced. She
shook her head. "Never mind. That's not important. If she was
blackmailing people, that might be a reason for them to go after her.
Do you know who she was blackmailing?"

"No. I really don't. Maybe Andrew, since he was also... dating
her. Although..." Henry said, straightening. "Although, if I'm
honest, it wasn't so much dating as it was me taking her to fancy

restaurants. She was beautiful alright, but the more I think about it, the more I think… she really was a snake in the grass."

Wilma's eyes widened. "Oh? So that's why yesterday you said 'good riddance to bad rubbish' when you thought she had left us in the lurch? Did you two have a fight recently or something?"

Henry ran a hand through his hair. "Yes. Yes, we were always fighting. I'm sorry, Miss Wade. You must think I'm a terrible person. I date her, I buy her a ring, I want to break up with her, I speak terribly about her. It's just all so… confusing for me."

Confusing because he was lying?

Wilma patted his hand again and drank some of her tea as she processed this information. She had a delicate line to balance here. She needed him to believe that she believed him, so she could get more information about this. The blackmail angle was surprising and she needed to know if that was something he was making up, too.

"Henry, I know that this is difficult, but can you answer a few more questions?" she asked slowly. "I want to know more about this blackmail. If she picked the wrong person, they might have taken matters into their own hands, rather than pay her."

"I… don't have much to say about that," Henry muttered, looking at the table.

Considering how much he had to say about everything else, Wilma found that very suspicious. She took another sip of tea, then asked, "You said something about Andrew."

"Well, yes. But he might actually love her, too," Henry grumbled with a shrug. "Veronica would talk about him sometimes on our dates. She liked to boast about all the compliments he gave her. He has to be the reason why she was cast in the lead role in the first place."

As soon as he said it, he winced and inhaled sharply. Clearly, that was something he hadn't meant to let slip. Wilma took a moment to calm her racing heart before she casually asked, "What do you mean by that? She's quite well-liked in town. I thought Julia hired her because she would fill seats for the performance."

"That's what convinced Julia, yes. But they never liked each other," Henry said, then stood. "I'm sorry, Miss Wade. This is all too much. I must ask you to leave now."

"Of course. If you need anything, let me know."

———

Detective Fellow frowned at Wilma in her modest cottage. She'd just finished filling him in on all the details.

"So, Julia is a potential blackmail victim, leading her to cast Veronica despite their differences," Wilma said. "And Henry was definitely lying about a woman living with him. Two wine glasses from last night? The bottle of painkillers for menstrual cramps? I think he was lying about dating Veronica."

"I agree," Jason said with a nod. "The question is why? And how does any of this relate to the murder?"

CHAPTER FOUR

A PLATE of brownies sat untouched on Julia's desk. Wilma lingered just outside, frowning at the plate. It had been a good batch, and even though she had come in early to give Julia her plate, Julia still hadn't touched it. Maybe she didn't like brownies?

Julia, Jason, and Andrew were all in the office, talking. Jason knew Wilma was lurking nearby, but the two suspects—and they were suspects—didn't.

The high school theatre was almost dead today. It should have been a mess of activity as the crew prepared for tonight's musical performance, but everything had ground to a halt with Veronica's death. Only a handful of people were there to start putting things away since it seemed that the performance was permanently canceled. A few of the cast thought they should dedicate the performance to Veronica's memory and let Beth take on the lead as her understudy, but even more thought it would be a disrespectful thing to do.

"I told you, Detective Fellow," Julia said within her office, "I didn't lay a finger on Veronica. After our fight, I stepped outside. I needed a moment to breathe."

"Did anyone see you?" Jason asked.

Julia groaned. "I... I made sure nobody did. But I was near the cameras. I'm sure you'll be able to verify my story."

Jason made a humming noise in his throat, followed by the noise of a pen scratching on paper. "Can you tell me why you were so careful not to let anyone else see you leave the theatre?"

"I... I had a cigarette, okay?" Julia said, sounding both embarrassed and defensive.

"Julia!" Andrew's spoke for the first time since Jason asked to speak with them. "You told me that you'd given it up. We passed around the card and everything."

"I know, I know," Julia said. Wilma resisted the urge to peek around the corner to see if she looked as defeated as she sounded. "It's just all the stress lately. With Veronica constantly on my back about rewrites and then Beth begging me to put her in the play, it's just been too much! I've never had a production cause me this much headache."

Wilma rubbed her chin as she listened to the conversation.. She had thought that it was strange for the stage manager to have so much to juggle, but she had chalked it up to not knowing how these things worked. Was there more to the situation than met the eye?

"You could have come to me for help," Andrew said, sounding disappointed.

"How could I, when you were going through your own issues?" Julia said, but there was a guarded note to her voice that told Wilma there was something else going on as well. At the sound of a chair scraping the floor, like someone had just stood up, Wilma hurried a few steps away.

A little bit later, Julia exited the office, carrying the plate of brownies with her. Tears were in her eyes as she hurried into the back. Wilma waited a little bit, listening to Andrew and Jason, before she followed Julia back. Even though she was only a few minutes behind her, by the time Wilma arrived, Julia had demolished the entire plate of brownies.

"Oh, dear," Wilma said in surprise. "Oh, you really must be under a lot of stress."

Julia glanced at the empty plate guiltily. "First smoking and now this. I'm just going to undo all the progress I've made."

She slumped into a hard chair and put the plate on the floor. Her arms wrapped around her waist as Wilma came toward her, shaking her head sympathetically.

"Now, now. Just because you've had a bad day or week, even a month or longer, it doesn't mean you can't start again. It's about how we get ourselves back on track." Wilma sat in a nearby chair and patted Julia's shoulder gently. "Take it from someone who's seen more of the world. Mistakes don't have to be permanent."

Julia gave her a small smile. "It's just all so much. Veronica spent the last three weeks trying to bully me into paying for her performance, even though she knew coming in that we are a volunteer group for charity. Nobody was getting paid. It was the darndest thing."

Wilma thought about Henry and his accusations that Veronica was blackmailing people. "Julia, I've heard rumors that Veronica... well, that she was trying to force some people in the group to pay her. That she might have even resorted to blackmail."

"Did you?" Julia's eyebrows pinched together a moment before understanding blossomed on her face. "Oh! Oh, just a few days ago Veronica was telling me that she'd been looking through my old Facebook posts and found something 'interesting.' I was too busy to listen to her, but now that I think about it, she might have been planning on blackmailing me. Though what she could have found, I don't know."

"Veronica was causing a lot of problems, wasn't she? I never really understood what was happening between her and Beth," Wilma said, her eyebrows furrowing together.

Beth was also a major suspect, and if Julia really had been on camera during the window of Veronica's murder, then perhaps she could still give more tidbits on the other suspects. It was difficult to know exactly how deeply the conflict between Beth and Veronica went. When Wilma was delivering her brownies, she had been unable to find any address for the young understudy.

"Oh, the whole thing with Beth confuses me, too," Julia confessed. "You know the guitar solo in Act Two? The one the Beth was playing because otherwise she would have nothing to do?" Julia prompted.

Wilma nodded. "I quite enjoy that sequence. I think it's one of my favorite parts."

"Just in the last few days, Veronica has started to insist that she should play that solo, that it made more sense for her character to do it. She's been causing such a big fuss, even threatened to walk out of the performance entirely!" Julia shook her head, looking frustrated and upset. "I was trying to get to the bottom of it, but Veronica was never interested in explaining her reasoning."

Wilma nodded sympathetically. "And what about this business about the show last night and Beth's mother?"

"Oh. Yes, that." Julia shook her head as she fidgeted in her seat. "I had a feeling that Veronica was going to skip out on opening night just to screw us over. But when Beth approached me, suggesting that maybe she could take the premiere, Veronica was all over refusing that. Apparently, last night was the only night that Beth's sick mother could come see the performance."

"It seems like it would be quite a big deal to switch out the entire performance."

"I was trying to see if Veronica would let Beth take the scenes when the character was younger," Julia explained. "Just so she could have a larger role for tonight. Veronica flatly refused, and was once more insisting on taking that guitar solo."

Wilma processed the pieces of the puzzle. If Beth wanted her sick mother to enjoy the performance, killing Veronica would certainly ruin that. "Why did Veronica dislike Beth so much?"

Julia cleared her throat. "It's probably Henry. He and Beth were together for a while, and Veronica wanted him."

"Henry said he was seeing Veronica," Wilma said in surprise.

Julia frowned. "He was? Really? He never told me."

The pieces were clicking together in Wilma's mind, but the big picture was still missing. "Do you know where I can find Beth? I wanted to talk to her and give her some goodies," she said. "But I couldn't find any address in the volunteer's booklet."

"I don't really know where she lives," Julia admitted. "But she works at the café, so you might be able to catch her there."

"Thank you, Julia," Wilma said, patting the other woman's knee. "You've been a massive help. And keep your chin up. Jason Fellow is a dogged detective, but he is good at what he does. He's fair about it, too. I can assure you that he'll find the real killer."

Was it just Wilma's imagination, or did Julia not look very reassured by that statement?

———

With a fresh plate of brownies, Wilma went to the café. There, she found Beth working at the cash register. When Wilma brought the brownies to the register, Beth looked at them and back at Wilma.

"I'm sorry, you can't bring outside food into the café," she said, all professional.

"They are for you, dear. Do you mind if we talk a little?" Wilma asked, smiling in her most motherly way. After a career of teaching, she knew how to make herself seem friendly and approachable.

Beth pulled her sleeves over her hands and nodded. She got one of her coworkers to take the register and led Wilma into the back. The heat from the ovens invaded the staff room and Wilma fanned herself.

"I was just wondering if you were alright," Wilma said gently. "This has all been a rather frightening experience. I just wanted to ask you about a few things I'd heard about you and Veronica... and Henry," she added, carefully watching Beth's face.

"Don't know what you could have heard, but go ahead," Beth said.

Before Wilma could actually start asking questions though, a timer in the kitchen went off. Beth hurried away. Wilma sighed, sitting down to wait—only to jump back to her feet when Beth let out a sharp cry. She raced after the younger woman to find her kneeling on the floor, a baking tray half in the oven and a dozen fresh-baked cookies scattered on the floor. Beth held her hands before herself as shiny, red burns slowly started to blister on her palms.

"Call the hospital," Wilma called to one of the other workers as she hurried to Beth. "Let's get your hands in some cool water. What happened?"

"It was stupid," Beth whimpered. "I grabbed the tray with my bare hands. Stupid, stupid!"

Wilma ran cool water and had Beth put her hands in the stream. She wouldn't get anymore questions answered today, it seemed.

CHAPTER FIVE

THE NEXT DAY, the whole cast was brought back together so that Julia could give them all the bad news. It was officially decided that the musical presentation was cancelled. Many people nodded their agreement while others shook their heads. Wilma was of two minds about the whole thing. It seemed a waste of all their time and money, but she understood needing to be respectful of Veronica's memory at this time.

As the cast dispersed to deal with the cleanup and storage of props and scenery, Wilma made her way to Andrew. He looked downcast, upset, but not in the same way that the others did. He was the only one of the suspects left that she hadn't been able to speak with.

"Are you alright, Andrew?" Wilma asked sympathetically.

Andrew jumped and turned to her. "Oh, Miss Wade. I apologize, I was lost in thought. I... I think I'm alright. Thank you. It's just all so tragic. Veronica and I were finally going to..."

He trailed off.

Wilma waited a moment then prompted, "Finally going to marry?"

"No. Well, yes. Maybe. You know I was planning to propose to her. But we were going to have our big break. Veronica had gotten a prominent role in a city theatre. She was taking me with her. We were going to go start rehearsals today, but without Veronica, they don't want me anymore."

Wilma frowned at him. "Starting rehearsals today? But what about the performance here in Barwick?"

Andrew grimaced. "Uh… well, see, that's just the thing. We weren't exactly planning on staying for the performance. I mean, I could have come back for my part. But…"

But it also meant that Veronica was planning on turning the Barwick production on its head for her own ends. Wilma shook her head in amazement. "Veronica was a very selfish woman, wasn't she?"

"It's not selfish! She had to think of her career," Andrew protested.

Henry, who had wandered nearby during the conversation, snorted. "We would have been better off if Veronica was never asked to be part of it. Beth is a much better actress, and she still could be leading lady, even with those injuries on her hands. We're making a mistake by closing the production now."

Andrew turned toward him, his expression incredulous. "Are you kidding me? Beth is terrible! She has no voice and she has one-note acting. She never should have been cast as the understudy in the first place, let alone as a leading lady."

Uh oh. Wilma looked between the two men, nervous as they started to glare at each other. "Gentlemen, while it's admirable that you're defending the ladies, how about we take it down a notch?"

They ignored her. Henry shook a finger in Andrew's face. "Beth is a wonderful actress. Veronica was always over the top and never allowed for any nuance in her performances."

Andrew threw his head back and laughed. "It's much better that we've completely shut down the performance rather than let Beth be our lead actress. It would have been even more of a disaster! Our audience would be so disappointed that they would be demanding that we refund them and give them back even more money. This was meant to be a charity to raise money, not a charity to wannabes."

Wilma lifted both her hands, not liking this turn. Tempers were running hot, but this was something else entirely!

"How dare you!" Henry shouted. "How dare you speak that way about her? Beth is magnificent! She was perfect for this role and she would have been a much better casting. Veronica only got famous because of her name and a few lucky breaks. Now she was trying to squeeze out everyone else. You're lucky, Andrew. Lucky that she died before she tossed you aside."

"You—" Andrew lunged but Wilma quickly put herself between the two men. They both jerked to a stop, staring at her as though they had forgotten they weren't the only ones in the theatre.

Wilma gave them her best teacher look. "That's enough, both of you! You should be ashamed of yourselves. Andrew, go take care of your performers. Henry, you come with me and calm yourself down."

She strode off, hoping that the two men would listen to her. To her relief, Henry followed after her, moving slowly as though he was ashamed of himself. Good. He should be! That sort of behavior was so immature. And he had been on the brink of attacking Andrew. Could he have gotten violent with Veronica, too?

Once they were alone, Wilma turned to him. "I am going to ask you a few questions, Henry, and you are going to be honest with me."

Henry, shame-faced, nodded.

Wilma put her hands on her hips. "Why were you pretending to date Veronica when you are so clearly in love with Beth? She's living with you, isn't she?"

It made sense. There were two wine glasses in Henry's kitchen and the place was decorated with a feminine touch. There was also no address listed for Beth in the volunteer registry. Clearly, they were trying to hide the fact that they were together. But why?

Henry's shoulders slumped. "Yes. Beth and I are together. Beth thought it would be best if we pretended like I was single, so I could get closer to Veronica."

Surprise rippled through Wilma. Her eyes widened as she processed this information. "Whatever for?"

Henry shifted on the spot, looking up, then down, then left, then right. Anywhere but directly at Wilma. She waited patiently, still confused about this whole turn of events. Finally, Henry met her eye as though hoping she would have gotten bored. When she stared at him steadily, he winced.

"When we heard that Veronica was going to be the leading lady, we realized that her reputation would be enough to lure a talent scout to Barwick for the performance. I pretended like I wanted to get close to Veronica so that I could push her into abandoning the production on opening night. It wasn't Beth's sick mother that would be in the audience, it was the talent scout."

Wilma's jaw dropped. "That is a lot."

Henry nodded miserably. "We were hoping that with Veronica dropping out, the talent scout would be able to see how good of an actress Beth is. She has such a hard time getting out of Barwick to auditions. We thought this might be the chance for her big break."

"And then Veronica insisted on performing for the premiere?" Wilma prodded.

"She found out about it somehow. She told me that she'd seen through me from the start and that an upstart like Beth would never get anywhere without hard work." Henry passed a hand over his face. "And then all that happened... and it was all for nothing in the end."

The whole plan seemed rather strange and convoluted to Wilma. They would have been much better off if Beth put in more effort to landing roles, she thought. Or at the very least, if Henry had used his position as leading man to get her a larger part in the play, rather than this strange sabotage.

But then, perhaps it was because Wilma didn't really understand how the theatre worked.

"What was the plan for if the talent scout left as soon as he found out that Veronica wasn't performing?" she wondered aloud.

Henry grimaced. "I never said it was a good plan. But it doesn't matter anymore, not with Veronica dead."

He walked away then, going back to the cleanup. Wilma couldn't get him or Andrew alone again. She signaled Jason, and after the production team was done with all the cleanup, they lingered behind to talk. The theatre was a ghostly place when it was empty. Julia gave Wilma the key to lock up after Wilma told her that she needed to sit and rest a little bit.

Jason and Wilma sat in the front row on the faded red-velvet chairs. Detective Fellow sighed as he stretched his legs out in front of himself.

"I haven't gotten much from the cast," he said. "Just rumors and gossip. Not many people want to talk to a cop about this business. Have you had any better luck?"

Wilma nodded. "I've learned quite a bit. First, Veronica and Andrew were dating. They had plans to abandon the musical performance for a gig in the city. Second, Beth and Henry are dating. They had plans to lure a talent scout to the performance and swap Veronica with Beth, so that Beth could get her big break. Veronica found out and was refusing to let Beth perform, even though Veronica didn't want to do it. Veronica also seemed to be blackmailing people, but I haven't learned anything about that line," Wilma admitted.

Detective Fellow shook his head. "If she was blackmailing people, it wasn't for money. I checked her financials. All the incoming money matches payments for jobs. I suspect that Veronica was killed for some mix of personal and professional motives."

"But the question is, why? And who did it?" Wilma shook her

head, frowning. "Would you like to come by my place so we can keep discussing the case? I can make more brownies and—"

She cut off suddenly as the image of her old, worn-out oven mitts came to her mind. They were in rough shape but she was loathe to get rid of them, as they had been a gift from her late fiancé. They had served her well for these many, many years that she had had them.

"Miss Wade? Wilma?" Detective Fellow prompted. "Are you alright?"

"Oh, I'm fine, dear." Wilma tapped her chin. "I think I know how we can prove who our killer is."

CHAPTER SIX

WILMA AND DETECTIVE Fellow found Beth at Henry's house. She answered the door with a pained expression, her hands heavily bandaged. Wilma winced in sympathy, remembering the shiny red burns that had been on her fingers and palms.

"Miss Wade. Detective." Beth looked from one to the other. "What can I do for you?"

"How are your hands?" Wilma asked, nodding toward the bandages.

Beth looked down. "Fine. The doctors think I'll recover quickly."

"It's strange, don't you think? You work at a café. We talked with your manager. You often are responsible for taking things out of the oven," Wilma said, folding her arms over her chest. "Nobody who works with baked goods regularly is going to forget to put on oven mitts before they take something out of the oven."

"I was just so distressed by everything that's happening, I guess I just wasn't thinking," Beth answered defensively.

Here, Detective Fellow spoke, his voice rumbling. "Or did you burn your hands on purpose to hide a different injury?"

Beth's face paled. "I don't know what you're talking about."

"I remembered how you pulled your sleeves over your hands at the theatre after Veronica was found, and again at the café," Wilma said. "And then you burned your hands in a way that a professional baker would never do. You were hiding the cuts on your palms, where the guitar string cut into you when you strangled Veronica Lane with it."

"I… that's ridiculous!" Beth cried.

Detective Fellow shook his head. "I don't think it is. Miss Wade has some theories. Why don't you share them, Miss Wade?"

Wilma nodded. "Veronica was very hard on you. She used every opportunity to put you down. She even went so far as to try to take your guitar solo from you, even though she hadn't practiced it at all in her performances. Then there was the business with Henry. Your boyfriend who you told to start going on dates with Veronica, as a means to manipulate her."

Beth scoffed.

"But you weren't expecting Henry to be quite as good of an actor, were you?" Wilma continued. "You started to wonder if maybe he wasn't actually falling for her. Add to it all the professional rivalry and there started to be some personal jealousy going on. You hated Veronica for everything she had that you thought you deserved."

Beth's jaw worked. "I've been working my butt off since I was fifteen. Full-time school and full-time work. When was I supposed to go have the manicures and auditions and the dinner and drinks with producers that she had? Her parents got her the first job she had acting, did you know that? She was handed everything on a silver platter and then pretended as though it was only 'hard work' when she never worked a real job in her life."

Wilma gazed with sympathy at Beth. "It's hard to be rejected, especially when it's something you're passionate about." She thought about the many rejects she had gotten from her writing and sighed. "But that doesn't justify what you did. She drove you to the breaking point, but your emotions were yours to handle. You chose to blame her for everything, rather than to find a different way to do things."

"You don't know what it's like! She was deliberately blocking me. She had everything and didn't deserve any of it!" Beth's eyes glimmered with tears. "She tormented me from the time we were in elementary school. She taunted me, telling me how useless I was. Then she started talking about Henry. She'd decided to take him from me. She didn't even like him. She told me that she thought he was pathetic. But she was going to take him just because she could. Like she'd taken everything else!"

Beth shook, her jaw clenched. Tears shone in her eyes as she looked wildly from Wilma to Detective Fellow.

"And so that's why you killed her? Because you were certain Henry would fall for her?" Jason asked, his voice low.

Beth's shoulders slumped. Her jaw worked but the understanding that she had already confessed slowly dawned in her eyes. "I didn't plan to. Even after I grabbed that guitar string, I just wanted to scare her. At least, I thought I did."

Wilma shook her head slowly. "It must have taken a lot of rage to strangle Veronica. Was it worth it, Beth? Was it worth the pain that you inflicted on her family?"

"I didn't mean to hurt anyone but Veronica. I hated her. I'm not even sorry that she's dead. But I am sorry that the production was shut down. It could have done a lot of good," Beth murmured.

Wilma was shocked. The past murders that she had helped Detective Fellow solve never made it easier when the murderer spoke like this. The utter disregard for the human life that had been ended made Wilma's stomach churn. She understood motives. The desperation and insecurity, the thirst for recognition. The feeling that someone didn't deserve what they had.

But this was unlike anything she'd witnessed before. It wasn't even about the money, it was all just that Beth had decided

Veronica was personally responsible for the ills Beth faced. It was tragedy in its finest form.

"Veronica Lane didn't deserve to be murdered," Wilma said.

Beth smiled bitterly at her. "You're only saying that because you didn't know her."

Detective Fellow pulled the handcuffs off his belt. "Beth Calloway, you are under arrest for the murder of Veronica Lane."

Beth's eyes flooded with tears. She didn't resist as Jason put the handcuffs on her, but there was a petulant look in her eye as he started to lead her away.

"I just wanted to get some recognition," Beth said as Jason pulled her to the police cruiser. "Nobody cares about hard work anymore. It's all about who you know. Veronica Lane didn't deserve the success she got. I did!"

———

Later, Wilma left the police station after reporting everything that she had figured out. Beth's confession was a matter of record now. The case of Veronica Lane had been closed, but Wilma didn't feel the same satisfaction at catching a killer as she had in the past. The case had been so tragic in the end. There had been such a web of lies and betrayals, of secrets, jealousy, and ambition.

As she walked to her car, she gazed at the bright spring flowers that lined the stationhouse. In a time of new life and possibilities, it seemed even darker that someone's life had been cut short.

"Wilma," Detective Fellow called after her.

Wilma paused and let the young detective catch up with her. He gave her a concerned look as he came trotting up next to her. It had been a long, hard day, and she could see her age reflected in his eyes. Wilma smiled at him. Some people acted as though she was helpless and frail, but Jason always treated her with respect. His concern wasn't because he saw her as old, but rather because she was his friend.

"I wanted to thank you again for your help on this case," Jason said as they walked together. "Let me buy you dinner. I don't know about you, but I'm bushed and I don't relish the idea of having to cook a meal tonight on top of everything else."

Wilma thought about her nearly-empty fridge. She had been so caught up in her writing and the musical production that she had been neglecting shopping. She agreed to the dinner and they headed for the café together. There, they ordered soup and sandwiches and took a booth near the window.

"So, here's another Barwick mystery solved," Jason said as they waited for the server to bring them the food. "Beth is going to be prosecuted to the full extent of the law. I still didn't find anything about Veronica's supposed blackmailing schemes. But maybe that's a mystery for another time, huh? We've done quite enough for one day."

"I agree. I think that the whole blackmail thing was made up, really," Wilma said casually. "To lead us off track."

But really, she filed it with the poisoned chocolate egg from Easter. They may have solved Veronica Lane's murder, but there was a larger mystery under the surface of Barwick, one that wasn't quite so easily solved.

"That reminds me, do you have more of those delicious brownies?" Jason asked hopefully.

Wilma shook her head. "No, I don't have any at the moment. But I'll be more than happy to make some more tomorrow."

Jason smiled his thanks. The food was served and Wilma started with her soup. It was delicious and creamy. For a while, they ate in silence, both too busy sating their hunger to pay much attention to anything else.

"I'll tell you what," Wilma said finally. "I'm never going to volunteer for something like that again."

Jason grinned. "That reminds me. There's going to be a library book sale and I thought you might like to—"

Wilma threw her napkin at him.

Jason laughed. "Okay, okay! I won't give them your name, then."

They started to laugh as the spring sun slowly set over Barwick. Another mystery had been solved. And as for the larger mystery at play... well, Wilma Wade was still on the case.

The End

MURDER AT THE LAKE

A SMALL-TOWN SUMMER COZY MYSTERY
WITH A SENIOR SLEUTH

CHAPTER ONE

WILMA WADE MOVED to Barwick after she retired as a school teacher, intending to live out the rest of her life in the peaceful solitude of a small town and all the personalities that came with it. Barwick, however, kept dropping murders into her lap. It was dreadfully incontinent for the simple life, but it was quite exciting for a mind as sharp as Wilma's.

On this bright July day, the only murder on her mind was the thought of picking up a hammer and smashing the bead that, no matter how she twisted it, would not stay on the hemp twine that had been provided.

"This thing hates me," she said sadly as Liv joined her. She had said her last name, but Wilma had been too busy trying to capture the beads that escaped as soon as she put her purse on the table, knocking over the container they were in.

Liv, a young woman with mouse-brown hair and lovely brown eyes, smiled warmly at Wilma. "Then you got to sweet-talk them. Come here, you little beauty," the younger woman crooned as she got the bead in place. With a few deft movements, she had secured it.

Wilma shook her head in amazement.

She'd heard about the annual July Friendship Festival by the Lake, a weekend-long celebration that the Barwick Artisan Guild hosted every year. There were games, contests, and so many different art classes that it made Wilma's head spin. Though there were drop-in activities available, Wilma had splurged on renting herself a private cabin and spending the whole weekend at the festival.

Strictly speaking, Wilma lived a conservative life. Her little cottage was just big enough for one person, and she kept everything neat and orderly. The items she kept were either useful or deeply sentimental. If there was one thing Wilma Wade could not stand, it was clutter—knickknacks and trinkets had no place in her world.

Which made it all the more ironic that, on the first morning of the Festival, she found herself seated at a friendship bracelet workshop, threading beads onto colorful twine. It wasn't the kind of thing she'd usually keep, but maybe—just maybe—a handmade token shared with someone she loved could count as sentimental. At least that's what she told herself as she chose her first bead.

"There you go," Liv said, handing the twine and bead back to Wilma. "That should keep it in place. Who are you making your bracelet for?"

"If I can get them to behave, I want to make matching bracelets for myself and my cousin, Martha," Wilma explained. She selected another bead and slid it onto the twine. Both it and the first one stayed in place.

"There, see?" Liv grinned at her. "If you need any further help, just flag me down, okay?"

"Can't you just ignore your other students and talk me through it all again?" Wilma joked. She laughed at the concerned look on Liv's face. "Never mind, dear. I can manage."

Liv chuckled nervously as though she still wasn't sure if Wilma was being quite serious. She moved off. Wilma sorted out the beads she wanted for the bracelets, then carefully started a second one, to make sure she got all the beads in the same order. The second bracelet started much easier than the first, with that foundation bead staying in place.

Wilma looked up, feeling rather proud of herself. Liv had moved to one side of the dozen or so tables that were set up with the beading equipment. She was talking with another of the artisan instructors. Emma, was it? Liv's back was to Wilma so she couldn't see her face, but Emma frowned deeply. She lifted a hand to wag a finger in Liv's face, the gesture surprisingly aggressive.

Liv stepped back and Emma walked away. That was the end of it. No raised voices, nothing except a brief conversation. Wilma's instincts were on guard. What had that been about? Wilma hesitated as she watched Liv go back to her own project. The instructor seemed upset, but not overly shaken. Was it really her place to start prodding and poking?

Well, what was the point of being known as the retired-teacher, amateur writer, unofficial sleuth if she couldn't prod a little? It was all probably nothing but Wilma didn't want to take any chances. She glanced around. There were two teenagers down at the other end who were more interested in gossiping about high-school than paying attention to Wilma. She deliberately undid the foundation bead of her second bracelet and lifted her hand in the air as the beads scattered over the ground.

"Miss Wade, let me help you," Liv said, taking a seat next to her at the table.

"Thank you, dear," Wilma said, patting her arm. "I tried to do that sweet talk thing, but it just won't work for me. Do you mind terribly if you sit with me? I'm afraid that while it might be possible to teach old dogs new tricks, they require a bit more patience."

Liv laughed and nodded as she fixed the foundation bead. "Of course, Miss Wade. I'm happy to help. But if anyone else needs me, I'll have to see to them, too."

"Of course." Wilma nodded. From experience, she knew asking

directly about the tiff with Emma would end with Liv just brushing it off. She needed to build a rapport first, so Wilma cast her mind about for a conversation starter. "You know, this weekend is quite the splurge for me. I don't usually do this sort of thing. I'm not much of an artist. Never have been. But I thought I should do something outside of my comfort zone."

"You don't have to be an artist to create and enjoy the process of art," Liv answered.

Wilma hummed, uncertain about that. "I'm not so sure that the process of art is that enjoyable when you look at your final project and dislike it."

"I always find little things that are wrong with my finalized pieces, too," Liv said with a shrug. "The trick is to enjoy the act of creativity, and to remember that you have to practice to get better. Even Leonardo Da Vinci and Vincent Van Gogh disliked their own work."

"That doesn't sound right," Wilma said.

Liv grinned at her. "It is! I've done all sorts of research into art history."

It still didn't really sound right, but Wilma supposed even if Liv was lying, it was coming from a good place.

"My friend was the one who put me up to it," Wilma continued, smiling as she thought of Detective Jason Fellow. "I recently had a short story accepted by a magazine and he insisted I do something special for myself. I decided to come here and try it out. The lake is lovely and the cabins are quite nice."

Liv grinned. "That they are. If you ever want to go out onto the lake, there are canoes that you can get. You just need to find one of the organizers and have them unlock the shed. It's always lovely out on the water."

"Oh, I don't know about that. I'm not much of a swimmer, either!" Wilma laughed as she strung a few more beads on both her bracelets. She admired the way Liv strung her friendship bracelet, noting the teal and turquoise beads she picked. "You have lovely taste."

"Thank you. I—" Liv cut off abruptly, her jaw clenching as her eye narrowed at an approaching figure.

"Excuse me," Liv said in a huff. She stood and headed for the newcomer, a woman with red hair. "Kat. What are you doing here?"

"Is there a reason I shouldn't be?" Kat asked, flicking her red hair over her shoulder. "I'm pretty sure the activity sheet said 'everyone welcome.' I'm part of everyone, aren't I?"

Liv pinched the bridge of her nose. "I really don't need to deal with you today. Why don't you go bother someone else, Kat? Seriously. I don't know why you would even show up here."

"I showed up here because Cari asked me to," Kat spat back. "In case you haven't noticed, Liv, you're not the center of the universe."

Cari? That was the project coordinator. Wilma watched, fascinated. First Liv had that argument with Emma, and now Kat. Was she the sort of woman who smiled at people while stabbing them in the back? Was that why she was having two arguments in the span of half an hour?

A young, plump woman with curly hair rushed over. "Kat! I'm so glad you could make it. Liv, I asked Kat to come help me out with a few things."

Liv frowned, but shrugged. Cari and Kat walked away, but the redhead turned and glared at Liv a few times. For her part, Liv was in a distracted, surly mood after that. Wilma knew better than to ask now. It could wait until tomorrow.

———

The next morning, Wilma woke bright and early. She made herself a cup of coffee and headed outside of the little cabin, thinking that a nice walk along the lake sounded like an excellent way to start the morning. As she headed down the crisp path, she spied something in the water. It was a canoe that had tipped over and half-floated near the shore.

And next to the canoe was a body, face-down in the water. Red hair rippled around the woman like waves of fire.

CHAPTER TWO

DETECTIVE JASON FELLOW rubbed sunscreen onto his red nose as he headed from the parking lot to the lake. Wilma shook her head when she saw how sunburned he already was. She told him he needed sunscreen before he went hiking last week. Jason might be a clever detective, but he had made quite the mistake by not listening to her.

"What do we have?" he asked as he joined Wilma. She had made sure to stand watch over the scene, preventing anyone from moving the body other than to pull it out of the water. The muddy shore would hopefully yield some useful prints.

"The victim's name is Katrina Johnson," Wilma answered. "She wasn't registered for the weekend, but joined a few drop-in classes yesterday."

Detective Fellow carefully observed the scene and ordered the forensic team to do what they needed so he could get a closer look at the body. Something on the victim's wrist caught Wilma's attention and she pointed at it.

"Is she wearing a bracelet?"

Jason knelt beside the body and checked her wrist. "Yes, she is. Why? Is it important?"

"It might be. Can I get a closer look at it?" Wilma asked.

Jason carefully removed the bracelet as Wilma put on a pair of gloves, then handed it over. Once it was in her hand, Wilma recognized it. The turquoise and teal beads were distinctive.

"This is the friendship bracelet that Liv was making in her class yesterday." Wilma held the bag up to inspect it more closely. "What's strange is that Kat showed up at the class and she and Liv had a heated discussion. It was clear Liv didn't want her there. Later in the day, I saw the two of them with Cari, the event coordinator, and none of them looked happy. So how did Kat end up with a friendship bracelet Liv made?"

Jason ordered the team to take Kat to the waiting ambulance, which would in turn take her to the morgue. They covered her with a cloth before leaving. Wilma watched them go, her heart heavy. It was a terrible thing for such a young person, someone with so many possibilities in their future, to end like this.

"Which ones are Liv and Cari?" Jason asked Wilma.

There was a small crowd near the cabins. Many of them looked over in this direction curiously, but most of them were listening to Cari speaking.

"Cari is the one at the front wearing pink," Wilma answered. "And Liv is off to the side in blue."

Jason nodded. "You think that Kat stole the bracelet?"

"I'm not sure what to think. I just know that this doesn't really make sense. What was Kat doing here at night?" Wilma wondered aloud.

Jason adjusted his cap and turned so the sun wasn't so direct on his red cheeks. "I'll be honest, Miss Wade, I'm not sure there is anything to investigate here. On the surface, it looks like Kat took a canoe out on the lake without a lifejacket and capsized. Tragic, but not a crime."

Wilma turned to him with a frown. "You think it was an acci-dent?" She glanced at the forensic team. "Hmmm."

"I said it looks like an accident," Jason corrected. "But you're right that there is just enough suspicion about this scenario that I'm not going to rule anything out. Right now, the working theory is that she was staying with someone overnight here, then went out in a canoe, possibly drunk. She smells very strongly of wine. It's possible she hit her head and went overboard."

Wilma shook her head. "There weren't any obvious injuries on her head, though."

"True. She might have just been so drunk she passed out." Jason tapped his chin thoughtfully. "Maybe someone was with her. Maybe something happened and that person panicked and set the scene. I'm not ready to call it a homicide, but I'm also not ruling it out. I'll order tests to check for alcohol and drugs in her system."

"That is a good idea," Wilma said, nodding. "In the meantime, you should know that the canoes are kept locked. You'll want to talk to Cari about who had access to them. If Kat did go out onto the water, whether by herself or someone else, someone would have had to help her get the canoe. It might be useful to establish a time of death."

"Astute as always, Miss Wade," Jason said, grinning at her.

Wilma rolled her eyes and blushed. It was difficult for her to accept praise, even when she knew Jason was perfectly sincere. Wilma considered herself to have lived a perfectly comfortable but unre-markable life, and she was happy to say that it had been a good life, indeed. She wasn't looking for notoriety or fame in her golden years.

"That said, I have something else to talk to you about." Jason's expression grew more serious. He looked around to make sure they were alone and led Wilma a little further from the other police. "I went to take another look at the Easter case and discovered that the chocolate egg that you'd been given is missing."

"The egg?" Wilma repeated, stunned.

Last Easter, a prominent resident of Barwick had been poisoned. In the course of the investigation, she and Jason had discovered that a chocolate egg given to Wilma had also been poisoned. The killer denied all connection with the egg, which had left Wilma off-balance for some time. Someone had tried to kill her, yet she was no closer to knowing who it was now than she had been way back in April.

"There's no sign of any foul play in the precinct, nothing to indicate someone broke in," Jason continued, his expression grave. "I've decided that, for now, I'm going to act as though I don't know what happened. I have a feeling that whoever came after you might try again."

Wilma shivered. If she had any idea about who could want her dead, maybe this wouldn't be so frightening.

"When was the last time you saw the egg?" she asked, trying to jumpstart her investigator's mind. No point in panicking if she could plan and learn instead.

"It's been a few weeks since I last looked at it," Detective Fellow answered. "I looked at the record logs and nobody else checked out the evidence. So either we had a break-in that nobody in the station knows about, or someone who works at the station checked out a different evidence box and snuck into this one in the meantime. I hate to think it might be one of my coworkers, but we don't have many suspects."

Wilma nodded her agreement. She watched the small crowd, hoping that anyone watching would just assume they were talking about Kat's death. It seemed almost morbid to be discussing the possibility that someone might be trying to kill Wilma after another woman just died.

"I don't think I've made anyone at the precinct angry, have I?" Wilma asked.

Jason shook his head. "I can't think of anyone who dislikes you on the force. So, we're most likely looking at someone who was bribed to steal it."

Wilma shuddered. "I don't suppose we can hope that a rat stole it and died in the walls somewhere?"

"There's no way for rodents to get into the evidence room, I'm afraid."

That was what Wilma had been afraid of. "I just keep thinking that it was only those smugglers, the ones sending exotic animals through Barwick, that could have the motive and means to do this. But they're all in jail, and would they really be so bent on revenge?"

"I've been thinking about them, too. Unfortunately, I haven't had any luck in trying to talk to them." Jason shook his head, his expression wary. "Keep your eyes and ears open, Wilma. If you hear or see anything suspicious, let me know. I'm available at any time. Don't think that you'll be disturbing me or any of that sort of nonsense," he added with a stern look. "No matter what time, you give me a call."

Wilma studied the young man, partly exasperated and partly touched. Over the time she had come to Barwick, Detective Jason Fellow had become quite a friend to her. She wasn't sure what her life would have been if he hadn't been such an open-minded young person. While other police might have written her off as a dodgy old woman, Jason had taken her seriously from the start.

"I'll be careful," she promised.

Jason nodded, sighing. "And that means you ought to steer clear of any possible danger."

"I understand that," she said dryly as she rolled her eyes.

"Which means I think you should avoid investigating the possibility of a crime happening," Jason said, a smile twitching his lips. "At least, until we know if a crime actually happened."

Wilma patted his shoulder gently. "But how will we know a crime happened if we don't investigate?"

CHAPTER THREE

DESPITE KAT'S death and the presence of the police, it was decided that the day's festivities would go forward as planned. Everyone at this point assumed that it was just a tragic accident. Except Wilma... and the killer, of course. Wilma observed her fellow Friendship Festival participants as she strode around the grounds. There was an air of nervousness and sadness at first, but this quickly gave way to gossip, and finally to people discussing their own lives and places within the festival.

Wilma's first activity that morning was a 'Friendship Round Table' which she quickly learned was actually more like friendship speed dating for anyone who came to the festival without a friend. It was the perfect opportunity to talk with lots of people and ascertain if anyone knew about the feud between Kat and Liv or had reason to kill Kat themselves.

"I don't even know who Liv is," most of the others said.

Needless to say, when the exercise was done, Wilma hadn't learned anything of importance. Nor had she come out of it with the possibility of a new friendship, either. Perhaps that was her mistake, but she didn't feel the need to develop any more close friendships in Barwick. She had plenty of people in the hospital where she read her short stories who were happy to see her, and if she ever needed anything, Jason and the other police were only a phone call away.

After that came to nothing, Wilma opted out of her next activity, string art, and instead went back to her cabin. There, she made herself a cup of tea and drank it slowly as she considered the events of yesterday. The mystery—and lack of answers thus far—weren't quite enough to distract her from the worrisome news that Detective Jason Fellow had left her with.

"The problem is, we don't know who poisoned that egg in the first place," she told her coffee cup. She had learned during the writing process that sometimes it was nice to say things out loud, it helped to figure out problems. "Lena Morgan was the one that gave me the egg and when we thought she had poisoned Tom, she disappeared. She wasn't the killer, but she still left that message."

Wilma paused as she remembered the hastily scrawled note Lena left behind before she disappeared. *I didn't mean to get involved. I didn't know. Please, don't let them find me.*

Even after Lena was found, she refused to say who 'they' were. Wilma hadn't seen anything about her since, though Jason promised he was keeping an eye on her. Now with the chocolate egg being stolen, maybe it was time they tried to get answers from Lena again.

Not that she could do that in the meantime. There hadn't been any attempts on her life since Easter, so Wilma decide she wasn't going to worry about it anymore. Instead, she was going to focus on solving the mystery of Kat's death before the trail went cold. With that in mind, she sought out the instructor Liv had had an argument with the previous day, Emma. Maybe she would know more about why Liv and Kat were so hostile to each other.

"Oh, I can answer that, alright," Emma said with a surprisingly smug grin on her face. She was cleaning up after an activity and Wilma started to help. "Liv and Kat grew up here in Barwick together, and they've been at each other's throats pretty much their entire lives. That said, it was really mostly on Liv's part. Kat was quite a sweet girl once you got to know her."

"Is that so?" Wilma asked politely.

Emma nodded. "She's quite a talented artist in her own right, too. I've long thought that she deserved to have more of a prominent role in the Artisan Guild. But there was this whole nasty business with Liv a few years back that completely ruined her chances."

Wilma swept some glitter into the garbage can, putting on her best 'excited for gossip' expression. "Oh really? What sort of nasty business was that?"

"I really shouldn't say," Emma said, glancing suspiciously around. She leaned in, her eyebrows drawing together in an expression of false worry. "If I'm honest, there really isn't any proof. It's all rumor."

"I won't tell a soul," Wilma promised.

Emma cast another obvious look around before she leaned in close. "Well, there was a big thing when Liv and Kat both submitted their artwork to a silent auction. Liv accused Kat of stealing several of her designs and ended up getting her kicked out of quite a few markets at the same time. It wasn't the only time Liv accused other artists of stealing from her as well."

"Oh, dear." Wilma put a scandalized hand to her heart. "How terrible!"

"Exactly. Liv has always thought she's better than everyone else."

Wilma shook her head, clucking her tongue. "Is that what you were arguing with her about yesterday? Liv, I mean."

"Arguing?" Emma shifted on the spot and looked away. "I don't know what you mean by arguing."

"Yesterday during the friendship bracelet class, I noticed you and Liv having words, just before Kat arrived," Wilma offered.

Emma blushed and cleared her throat. "Oh, well. Yes, we had a disagreement, but it wasn't an argument, really. I might not like Liv all that much but it's nothing personal against her. It's just clashing personalities. Yesterday was just one of those clashes. Don't think anything of it, we're squared away now."

"I see," Wilma murmured, not at all convinced.

"Yes. Well." Emma cleared her throat again. "I don't want to go around spreading rumors, but I do have to wonder about Kat's accident. It doesn't make much sense, you know. The whole thing. I heard the police talking about it, and I don't think… I shouldn't say this, but I'm not certain it was an accident."

Wilma straightened. She kept working, trying not to show how intrigued she was by Emma's statement.

"That's probably an awful thing to say," Emma added quickly. She bent her head and went back to gathering up the last of the art supplies.

"Why do you think that it's suspicious?" Wilma prodded. It was a tricky position to be in, learning more without being suspicious herself. "Did you see something last night?"

Emma put her box of supplies away and leaned forward, her eyes wide and earnest. "I just… the thing is, I don't think Kat was out on the lake by herself. Last night I heard voices outside of my cabin, and when I looked out my window, I saw two people getting into a canoe on the lake."

Wilma's heart pounded with excitement. Detective Fellow needed to know this right away! "What time was that?"

"Around midnight, I think."

"Did you see who was in the canoe with Kat?"

Emma shook her head. "If I'm honest, I'm not even sure that it was Kat. It was dark, I couldn't see anything clearly. I remember thinking that it was strange that anyone would want to go out on the lake that late, but I half-suspected it was a couple of teenagers being rebellious. I might have heard Liv's voice. But honestly, I couldn't tell you any more than that."

Wilma nodded. They finished cleaning up the space and Wilma sought out Liv. It was quite fortunate that Emma had seen what she had seen. If it was Kat and Liv out on the lake last night, that brought up a whole host of questions. Why would they go out on the lake so late at night, especially together, when they supposedly hated each other so much? And if it was them, how did Liv end up perfectly fine the next morning while Kate drowned?

Given that Kat was wearing the friendship bracelet that Liv made yesterday, the whole situation seemed even more suspicious.

Liv wasn't at the class she was meant to be teaching. Her co-instructor told Wilma that Liv wasn't feeling well and was in her cabin. Wilma swung by the kitchen to pick up a platter of cookies before heading to Liv's cabin. Liv answered the door with puffy red eyes. It was obvious she had been crying.

"Hello, dear," Wilma said kindly. "I heard you weren't feeling well, so I—"

"I'm sorry, Miss Wade." Liv rubbed her puffy eyes. "I appreciate you stopping by, but I really, really just need to lie down in a dark room for a while."

Wilma's eyes widened in surprise. "Oh. Well, have these cookies at least."

Liv took the cookies. "Thank you. I really have to go now. I hope you have fun with the day's activities."

She shut the door. Wilma headed back to the activities, her mind churning. That had been a rather abrupt end to the conversation. But more suspicious were Liv's tears. Why would she be crying over Kat's death if they really disliked each other so much?

CHAPTER FOUR

WILMA WENT to a watercolor painting class later that day. The sun was bright, the sky a brilliant blue, with fluffy clouds here and there. With the light reflected off the lake and the ring of vibrantly green trees around the water, it was the perfect image to paint. The class was set up beneath a large canvas tent and there were even a few fans set up in the space to help people keep cool.

Cari was one of the instructors for the class. Wilma noted that she looked rather withdrawn and pale, too, like Liv had been. Thinking about Liv made Wilma frown. Was her reaction to everything that happened a genuine shock? Or was it a guilty reaction? It was difficult to say, especially when Liv so rudely refused to talk with her.

Rudeness can come from many sources, Wilma reminded herself as she dipped her brush in a little bit of paint and washed it off in the water. It seemed counter-intuitive, but that was how you made the transparency of watercolors; you made a watery paint that you could then layer with.

"You're Wilma Wade, aren't you?" the grey-haired woman with sharp brown eyes sitting next to Wilma asked.

"I am. And you are?"

"Mary. Mary Collins-Smith." Mary offered a hand and Wilma shook it. Mary's grip was firm, her hands calloused.

Wilma nodded to herself. "You own one of the dairy farms outside of Barwick, don't you?"

"Yup. I've lived in Barwick all my life. Which is why I can tell you that I'm not surprised about what happened to poor Katrina last night." Mary shook her head, but her eyes were lit up with that particularly delighted look that came with good gossip. "She never stood a chance, not with her parents."

"Oh? What do you mean?" Wilma asked.

Normally, she wouldn't encourage blaming parents for how their children turned out, but with so little to go on so far, Wilma was going to take anything she could to start building her case. Knowing more about Kat's past could help to shed light on what happened.

"She and her family lived just down the street from me," Mary continued. "I always saw her riding around on that bike of hers. She would come to my place and climb into the fields to try to pet the cows. Nearly got herself killed too many times," she added, shaking her head. "Those parents of hers just didn't seem to care. She was always filthy and shoeless. Like I said, she didn't stand a chance. Poor child wasn't taught how to take care of herself. It's no wonder she ended up drowning herself in a stupid accident."

Wilma frowned as she painted mindlessly. "Do you know anything about her and Liv?"

"No," Mary said with a shrug. "But I thought I might have seen them together last night."

One of the ladies sitting on the other side of the table leaned forward. "I heard they were fighting yesterday. It wouldn't surprise me if it turns out Liv killed her. They were always at each other's throats, after all."

Cari headed over to them, her mouth pinched tight and fury in her eyes. "What is going on here? This is supposed to be an art class. Gossiping about what happened last night isn't going to help anyone. So please, let's stay on topic, shall we?"

Her eyes were slightly red, too. Wilma realized that Cari must have known Kat more than she was letting on. Wilma recalled seeing Cari and Liv talking and laughing the other day, in a way that suggested that they were more than casual acquaintances. If anyone was going to give her answers, Wilma knew it was Cari.

"I heard that the police are investigating Liv for murder," one of the women pipped up. "And that's why she's not allowed out of her cabin."

"That's not true," Cari said.

Wilma got to her feet. "May I say a few words on the matter? I often work with Detective Jason Fellow and I spoke with him about the unfortunate death as his team was processing the scene."

Cari hesitated but nodded once. She looked like she was on the verge of tears, poor girl.

"I know there is a lot of speculation happening over last night," Wilma said, turning to the group. "But when I talked with Detective Fellow this morning, he was not investigating a murder. There is currently no suspected foul play in Kat's death. The evidence as of right now points it to being an accident, and we should stay calm and not jump to conclusions on this matter. It's easy to see these things and think there is more going on than there is. The danger is making assumptions and judging a person guilty of a crime that might not even have been committed."

Even though she was convinced that there was foul play involved in Kat's death, Wilma didn't want to be responsible for a witch hunt. Her instincts weren't always right, and if it did turn out to be an accident, Liv deserved to be left in peace.

And if it was murder? So far there was no evidence that Liv had anything to do with it. It would be imprudent for the Friendship Festival to turn into the Liv is a Murderer Festival.

"So please, let's all just keep our heads and allow the police to do what they need to do," Wilma finished. "Thank you."

There were a few polite nods and everyone went back to their work. Wilma noted that Cari still seemed a bit shaken, though, so she suggested that they go to somewhere cooler so Cari could calm down a little easier. Cari agreed.

"I'm terribly sorry if it seems like I'm being insensitive to the events last night," Wilma told her once they were in a cabin. Wilma gave her some ice water. "You knew Kat, isn't that right?"

Cari nodded, sniffing. "She was a very dear friend. And Liv is also my friend. I hate hearing people talking as though she could have hurt Kat."

Wilma's eyes widened upon hearing that. "Oh? I was under the impression that Liv and Kat were at odds with one another. It must have been a difficult position to be in, being friends with both of them when they disliked each other so much."

Cari sipped her water as her eyes turned wet again. "You have no idea. It's been just awful. The three of us were the best of friends in elementary school right up into high school. We had all these plans to go to college together. It was going to be wonderful. We had all our lives planned out."

This news was especially surprising given how hostile the two women had been to each other. "My goodness," Wilma said, shaking her head. "What happened? I didn't interact with Kat that much, but Liv seems so sweet."

"She is, most of the time. But Liv, she can hold a grudge," Cari admitted. "And Kat, she was always bad at apologizing. Things had gotten strained because they weren't talking to each other and then they had this massive fight. I wasn't there but both of them told me about it, and I can't say either was in the wrong. Mostly, it was just because they were both so stubborn about it."

"What was their fight about?" Wilma asked.

Cari bit her lip and shook her head. "It doesn't matter. I had hoped that I could... you know, bring us all back together. I hoped so much. I really, really thought I could do it. I thought enough time had gone by and they'd both matured enough that maybe I could get them to talk it out again."

"Oh. Is that why you decided to help coordinate the Friendship Festival?"

"Yes. I convinced them both to come to the festival, like we used to when we were kids. I thought that if I could just get them remembering the good times, then maybe it would be enough. It's been difficult, trying to be friends with both and keeping them apart so they don't start fighting."

Wilma patted her arm sympathetically. In her life, she'd been in this sort of situation a few times. Sometimes, people just couldn't get along. Sometimes it was necessary to let go of old friendships. That was so much easier said than done, though, and it was quite heartbreaking when those choices had to be made.

"It was going so well," Cari murmured. "I really thought this time—"

She was interrupted by a knock on the door. Emma poked her head into the cabin, her gaze skipping over Cari to land on Wilma. "Miss Wade, Detective Fellow is here and wants to talk with you."

Wilma's heart clenched. Why would Jason be back so soon unless something had been found? She suddenly knew that this was officially no longer classified as an accident. Katrina had been murdered—the only question was, by whom?

CHAPTER FIVE

WILMA FOLDED her hands together as she sat down with Detective Fellow in her cabin. His expression was grim but not surprised. Just looking at him, Wilma had a good guess as to what he was going to tell her. The ME had found something suspicious about Kat's body.

"The toxicology report came back," Jason said, running a hand through his dark hair. "While Kat did have a pretty high alcohol content in her blood, it wasn't the only thing. She had a drug in her system that's commonly found in prescription sleeping pills. They're a kind of drug that has serious side-effects when combined with alcohol, and her levels were way higher than they would be if she had been taking prescribed medication."

"Oh, dear." Wilma pressed her fingers to her mouth. "That means Kat didn't have to hit her head to drown."

"She didn't even drown," Jason said grimly.

Wilma's eyes widened.

"The combination of the drugs and the alcohol are what killed her. The coroner found very little water in her lungs."

"And there's no way it could have been accidentally ingested?" Wilma pressed.

Jason shook her head.

That confirmed it, then. "So, it's murder."

"It might be, but not necessarily," Jason pointed out. "It's possible that Kat took both together on purpose, not knowing what the side-effects would be. It's also possible that she did it on purpose, knowing it would kill her. We don't have enough information yet to make that call."

Wilma nodded at the reminder. Even though her gut told her it was murder, she needed to stick with the evidence. It wouldn't help solve the case if she was running with a theory without anything to back it up. "And even if someone else is involved, that doesn't necessarily mean murder, either. It could be an accident. Someone who gave her the pills without knowing she'd been drinking, for instance, or maybe Kat ignored their warnings. Even if it was on purpose, that doesn't mean that the killer was trying to murder her."

"Exactly," Jason agreed.

Back on the same page, Wilma shared with Jason all she had learned about the rivalry between Liv and Kat. It was suspicious that she hadn't come forward to tell anyone that she had been on the lake with Kat—if it had been her at all. It was also strange that Liv would be so hostile toward Wilma when she came to talk to her.

"Although we need to remember that everyone has automatically assumed Liv has something to do with Kat's death, and understand that maybe she was just not in the mood for fending off accusations," Wilma said after she'd finished sharing everything she knew.

Jason nodded his agreement. "All the same, now that we have evidence that it might be murder, I better talk with this Liv. Especially about that friendship bracelet."

They headed to Liv's cabin. She looked at them suspiciously

when she opened the door, but the sight of Jason seemed to make her nervous. "What do you want?"

"I'm Detective Jason Fellow and I need to ask you a few questions about Katrina Johnson," Jason said professionally. "You knew the victim and were seen with her last night."

Liv lifted her chin, her gaze flickering to Wilma. "Why does it matter? It was a drunken accident, wasn't it?"

"It might be," Wilma said gently. "But we have evidence that indicates that it might not be an accident after all."

Liv's eyes widened. They darted from Wilma to Jason and finally she stepped back, opening the door to the cabin. "Come in," she murmured, sounding suddenly unsure. She shut the door quickly behind them and wrapped her arms around her middle. "What do you mean, it might not be an accident?"

Jason nodded to Wilma and she started to wander through the cabin, taking note of anything that seemed out of place. A bottle of wine sat on the table next to the small kitchenette and Wilma moved over to it. It had been opened recently, with what looked like a single glass emptied from it. Next to it was three clean wine glasses. What did Liv need three glasses for?

"We found a friendship bracelet on Miss Johnson's body," Jason was saying. "It appears to the be the same bracelet that you made during a class yesterday."

"It's not," Liv said shortly. "That has nothing to do with Kat's death. Why do you think it wasn't an accident?"

Wilma glanced over her shoulder at the two as she moved to the bed, which was tucked under a loft sitting space. Liv wasn't paying any attention to her.

"There were drugs found in Kat's system. Sleeping pills," Jason said.

A yellow prescription container caught Wilma's eye on the nightstand. She picked it up and read the label. "Sleeping pills exactly like these," she said, turning.

Liv jumped as she turned. Her eyebrows knit together as she

stared at the container. "Those? But those were in my suitcase. Kat wouldn't have gotten into those. She didn't believe in taking medications, either, so she wouldn't have…"

She trailed off, letting out a shuddering breath.

"So, she was here last night?" Wilma prodded gently.

Liv pressed her fingers to her temples as she sank onto a low bench. "Cari and Kat were both here last night. We used to be friends and last night, it seemed like maybe we could be friends again. It was like the old days, before everything went wrong. We were having a good time, making friendship bracelets and talking. Kat started to feel tired and decided to go back to her cabin around midnight."

"Kat didn't have a cabin registered," Wilma said.

"No, but we had a no-show who booked a cabin, so she was able to take it instead," Liv answered. "You can ask Cari. She stayed with me for a while longer before she left."

Jason nodded, making notes in his book. "And you all had wine?"

He nodded at the bottle near the sink.

"No. Only… only Kat did," Liv whispered.

Jason shared a look with Wilma. It was easy to make a guess as to one possibility that happened here last night. Liv pretended to make a peace offering and offered Kat a glass of wine, but slipped some sleeping pills into the drink without Kat knowing. Then it would be the combination of the drugs and alcohol that would kill her, and since Cari stayed with her, she would have an alibi.

Only… that didn't explain why Emma said she saw Kat with someone on the lake.

"Did you stay in your cabin afterward?" Wilma asked her. "Did you go out? We have a witness that says Kat was with someone on the lake."

"It wasn't me," Liv said, folding her arms over her chest. "After Cari left, I washed up and went to bed."

Jason hummed to himself as he inspected the bottle of wine. "And nobody can verify your whereabouts after she left?"

"No. Detective, I don't know how Kat could have gotten hold of my sleeping pills, but I didn't give them to her. You can't take them with alcohol. Kat and I might have had our differences in the past, but I didn't want her dead!" Liv ran her hands through her hair, tears spilling down her cheeks. "I don't know what happened, but I had nothing to do with it."

"I'm afraid I'm going to need you to come down to the station," Jason said firmly. "Is there anyone you would like to call?"

Liv stared at him with frightened eyes. "Are you arresting me?"

"Not arresting, no. I just need to ask you some more questions," Jason said, his voice growing gentle. "If you have a lawyer, I would advise you talk to them."

"I'm innocent. I don't need a lawyer," Liv insisted.

Jason lifted one of his hands in the air. "The innocent also need lawyers. They are there to advise you in matters of the law that you may not understand."

"Alright," Liv murmured. "I'll be out in a minute."

Jason and Wilma stepped out of the cabin. Wilma shook her head, not liking this turn. Even though there was this new evidence that pointed to Liv, her instincts told her Liv was telling the truth about reconciling with Kat. Why would she kill Kat right after starting to reconcile like that?

"I don't like it," she told Jason darkly. "It all just feels too neat without a real motive."

"I agree. I have a feeling we're going to find out this is a frame job," Jason whispered back.

Wilma gasped. "Someone is framing Liv? Why?"

"I'm not sure, only that it feels too neat and tidy. I need you to stay here and poke around some more," Jason told her. "I want to get Liv out of here so the killer thinks their plan worked and relaxes."

"So, we are assuming murder now?" Wilma asked, her voice low. "When did that change?"

Jason nodded back toward the cabin. "Since you found those sleeping pills so easily. No killer is that sloppy. Something else is going on here—and I need your help to figure out what it is."

CHAPTER SIX

AFTER JASON LEFT WITH LIV, Wilma went back into Liv's cabin. There were more answers here, she just knew it. But where to start looking? The wine bottle, maybe? Wilma picked it up and studied it. It looked like any other bottle of wine she'd seen. When she opened it and sniffed it, it smelled like wine. Nothing suspicious there. Though why Liv wouldn't put the opened bottle into a cooler or something, Wilma didn't know.

Nothing jumped out at her as suspicious, so Wilma sighed and moved to the window. From Liv's cabin, she couldn't see the lake. Or anything else, for that matter. Her cabin was the farthest from everything else, isolated against the trees. It would be easy for Liv to sneak out and back in without anyone noticing.

Wilma idly ran her fingers along the window frame, then paused when she met splintered wood. She peered a little closer and found the edge of the wood was slightly frayed. The way it would be if someone used something to slide between the window and the frame to unlock the hook-latch that kept it closed.

She left the cabin and searched around the outside. There weren't any footprints in the dirt, but just under the window, halfway up, was a smear of dirt. As if someone braced themselves against the wall to haul themselves through the window. Wilma whipped out her phone and took a picture of it, then headed back inside. Yes, there was some dirt and dust on the inside near the window, too.

Why would Liv sneak through the window of her cabin? She wouldn't.

Wilma straightened and sent a message to Jason, telling him about her findings. She took a few more pictures to send to him, then looked around the cabin with fresh eyes. Was there any other evidence that someone had been in here? She searched for a while but found nothing, though she did find a friendship bracelet, just like the one they'd found on Kat that morning, sitting on the floor near the nightstand.

So, Liv was telling the truth about that. Wilma took a picture of the bracelet and slipped it into a baggie and put it in her pocket.

The cabin wasn't offering up any further clues, so she headed out once more. Liv said Cari had been with her and Kat the previous night. That would be easy enough to verify.

She slipped out of the cabin and sought out Cari. Cari's eyes were wide, tears on her cheeks. She grabbed Wilma's wrist.

"Miss Wade, can I speak with you?" Cari sounded desperate.

"Of course," Wilma answered. "Let's go somewhere private."

Soon they were in the forest surrounding the lake. It was cooler in the shade, but Wilma still fanned herself. Cari twisted her hands, staring through the trees to the lake.

"What happened between Liv and Kat all those years ago?" Wilma asked.

"In high school, they were supposed to collaborate on an art project," Cari answered. "And they had very different ideas on how to do it. They were both stubborn and ended up deciding to just to their own projects instead. Liv's project ended up covered with paint and she blamed Kat. I know Kat didn't do it, but she wouldn't accept Liv's apology afterward. It all just ended up as a huge disaster."

"And they've been fighting ever since?" Wilma filled in.

Cari nodded. She turned back to Wilma. "I saw Detective Fellow take Liv away. She wouldn't have done this. Even when they were at their worst, she wouldn't have. Liv isn't that sort of person. Even with all her grudges, she wouldn't hurt anyone. She even agreed that Kat should come to the event after I told her that Kat was having some difficulties."

"Difficulties? What sort of difficulties?" Wilma pressed.

"I'm not entirely sure. I think she was having trouble with someone she was working with at an art gallery." Cari sighed. "Things were getting better between Kat and Liv. Last night, the three of us spent hours together. We talked and laughed and they were getting along. Liv apologized again for accusing Kat and Kat forgave her. Why would Liv do that if she was just going to kill Kat?"

Wilma pulled the friendship bracelet from her pocket. "Do you have one of these as well?"

Cari lifted her arm. A bracelet was wrapped around her wrist, just beside her watch. "We made them last night."

"I would like to take a picture, if you don't mind. It will help prove Liv's version of events," she added.

"Sure, go ahead." Cari held out her arm and Wilma snapped a photo, then took one with Cari's bracelet and the one she'd gotten from Liv's cabin together, to prove there were two of them. "Does Detective Fellow really think Liv killed Kat?"

Wilma knew she had to tread carefully. If she gave too much away, it might tip off the real killer that Jason knew this was a frame-up. While she didn't want to suspect sweet Cari, in truth they couldn't rule anyone out, not just yet. Cari might have decided that it was all getting to be too much and that the rivalry was out of control. She might have killed Kat and framed Liv to get them out of her life once and for all.

"Detective Fellow has to follow the evidence," Wilma answered. "Liv told us that you three went to her cabin, and Kat had some wine but you and Liv didn't. Why is that?"

"We'd drunk earlier, at my cabin."

Wilma's eyes widened. "At your cabin?"

Cari nodded. "That's where we started off. She and I were in my cabin and we had some wine, then Kat showed up. My bottle was empty so we went to Liv's cabin. We made the bracelets, but Kat started to say she was tired. We made plans to have breakfast together. I can't believe that this happened."

"I'm so sorry for your loss," Wilma said, patting her arm sympathetically. "It's a terrible thing. But there's something I don't understand. When Detective Fellow and I were talking to Liv, she didn't tell us that the three of you started at your cabin, Cari."

"She probably didn't think it was important." Cari sighed and shook her head. "But then, it could be that Liv doesn't trust police. She dated this police officer in college and it was a pretty toxic relationship."

"I heard that Liv and Kat were out on the lake together. Is it possible that, after you went back to your cabin, Liv went to see Kat? Or maybe Kat went back to Liv and they decided to go to the lake?" Wilma suggested.

Cari shook her head. "No. Not at all. Liv nearly drowned when she was ten and won't go in the water. She won't even take baths, she's too scared of it."

Then who did Emma see out on the lake? Wilma rubbed her chin thoughtfully. The pieces of the puzzle were there, but it wasn't quite coming together just yet. Especially since the drugs and wine would have killed Kat anyway. Liv would have known that. Why risk poisoning Kat in front of Cari, then set up such an elaborate scene?

"Cari, who all has the keys to the canoe shed?"

"Um... well, there's me, Liv, and Emma. Oh, and Jessica, who owns the campground." Cari stared at the lake again. "I can't think of how Kat would have gotten her hands on a key, or why she would go out on the lake in her state. But this whole thing... none of it makes sense. Why would anyone want to kill Kat?"

The inkling of an answer started to form in Wilma's mind. That was the rub, wasn't it? Nobody could think of any reason for why anyone would want to kill Kat. Even Liv had the flimsiest of reasons.

The poisoned chocolate egg from Easter came to Wilma's mind. It was strange for it to pop into her mind now of all times. There was no reason in this case to think that someone was going after her instead of Kat. But then... When Tom was poisoned at the Easter Parade, that was what tipped Wilma off to check the egg she'd gotten. It hadn't seemed connected, and yet she had nearly been poisoned that day, too.

What if a similar thing was happening here? Not targeting Wilma, no, but what if they were looking at this all wrong? What if they were trying to figure out who wanted to kill Kat... but maybe Kat wasn't the intended victim at all.

She pulled out her phone and typed a quick message to Detective Fellow. He needed to get back here right away.

"Miss Wade?" Cari asked, looking confused. "You look like you figured something out."

Wilma smiled at her. "I think I might have. Let's get back to the camp, shall we? I'm sure Detective Fellow will be here soon enough."

CHAPTER SEVEN

SEVERAL HOURS LATER, Wilma was in a class teaching how to create new covers for notebooks when Detective Fellow arrived. Everyone looked at him curiously, then started to whisper to each other when Wilma went to join him. She was almost done with her notebook and invited Jason to come join her. He sat next to her and they worked on the notebook.

"So did you pick up that bottle of wine like I asked?" Wilma asked. "I haven't seen you since this morning."

"You were busy when I stopped by again," Detective Fellow explained.

Wilma nodded her understanding. "So did you find what I thought you would?"

Jason's expression was grim, but a glimmer of hope lit in his eyes. "Yes. You were right. All we have left to find is motive."

"Then let's go find it," Wilma said bracingly.

They went to the necklace-making class, where Emma instructed the group. She paled when she saw them but tried to ignore them at first. Detective Fellow gestured her over and Emma whispered to the other instructor, then excused herself. Few people paid attention as she headed over to the Detective and Miss Wade.

"I'm in the middle of a class, can't this wait?" Emma asked, folding her arms.

"I'm afraid that in matters of murder, it can't," Jason answered. "You said you saw two people out on the lake last night, correct?"

Emma shifted from foot to foot. "Yes. But I didn't see who they were. I thought one of them sounded like Liv but I can't be sure."

"Can you tell me if they were in a canoe or just at the shore?" Jason asked.

"In a canoe. Have you arrested Liv?" Emma asked.

Wilma spoke up. "Are you sure they were in a canoe? On the water?"

Emma nodded, looking impatient. "Yes. I saw what I saw."

"Liv is deathly terrified of water," Wilma said. "And she, Kat, and Cari were drinking together last night. There's no way she would have gotten into a canoe, even during the daylight and sober. But that wasn't the only mistake you made, Emma."

Emma's eyes widened and she let out a short laugh. "A mistake I made? Miss Wade, what could you be getting at? I don't know what you're talking about."

"I'm talking about how Kat wasn't the one that you were going after. She died after ingesting the wine in Liv's cabin, wine that had had several sleeping pills crushed and dissolved into. But it wasn't meant for Kat. The killer hadn't intended for anybody except Liv to drink from the wine," Wilma said, putting her hands on her hips. "It was a risky plan. After all, how could the killer guarantee that only Liv would drink the wine? You didn't consider any other possibilities until after you saw Kat and Cari go into the cabin with Liv, did you?"

Emma fidgeted with her collar, looking away and back again. She pressed her lips together tightly. "I don't know what you're talking about. This is just one of your stories. Is this how you've supposedly solved all those cases? You just make up things and railroad innocent people?"

"You realized that you'd messed up and you needed to fix it," Wilma continued, ignoring the blustering accusations. "You couldn't go to the cabin and stop them from drinking the wine without giving yourself away, so you needed to make it look like an accident. So, you went to the canoe shed while they were in Liv's cabin and you set the scene. All you needed to do was to wait for the bodies to start dropping."

Emma let out a shuddering breath. "Detective, you can't believe what she's saying. It's all nonsense!"'

Detective Fellow's expression gave nothing away. "Please allow Miss Wade to finish."

A strange look came over Emma's face, as though she realized in that moment it was over. Her shoulders slumped and she turned back to Wilma almost reluctantly. Her jaw clenched but she nodded once.

"Fine. Go on," she said.

"When you realized that only Kat drank the wine, you decided to try to frame Liv," Wilma said. "But what I couldn't figure out was why. You and Liv had a bit of an argument the first day of the festival, but surely that wasn't enough for murder! But then I remembered what you told me about Liv getting Kat kicked out of artisan events."

Emma frowned. "What about it?"

"You said Liv had accused other artists as well, not just Kat," Wilma pointed out. "And so, I asked around. You were one of the artists she accused of copying her. You lost a huge commission with the town for public artwork because of it, didn't you?"

"The similarities between our submitted artworks were just a coincidence," Emma hissed, bright spots of anger rising in her cheeks. "I didn't steal anything. I didn't copy her."

Wilma nodded, though she wasn't sure she believed Emma. Either way, it didn't really matter. The outcome was the same. "But she ruined your reputation. You were ejected from the running to be part of the Guild leadership. It's taken you years to get back into their good graces, isn't that right?"

Emma's nostrils flared.

"You drugged Liv's wine with her own sleeping pills, hoping that it would look like an accident. But when Kat died instead, you decided to frame her. To ruin her reputation and bring her down," Wilma said, her voice growing steely. "Isn't that right?"

"You don't know what it's like!" Emma clenched her fists. "Everyone is so in awe of Olivia Weiss. She's not all that. She's a second-rate artist at best! She took everything from me just because I happened to borrow a few ideas. It wasn't fair! I'm a real artist. Not her."

Jason lifted one eyebrow. "So you decided to kill her."

Emma lifted her chin. "Yes, I did. I'm only sorry that Kat got caught instead of her. Kat was sweet. She didn't deserve to die. Liv did."

Detective Fellow pulled out a set of handcuffs. "You are under arrest for the murder of Katrina Johnson and the attempted murder of Olivia Weiss."

As Jason cuffed Emma and led her away, Wilma sighed. Another case solved. She enjoyed the feeling of the warm July sun on her face. It hadn't turned out to be much of a relaxing week-end... but maybe solving murders was an art in and of itself.

———

After Emma's arrest, Liv was released from police custody. She and Cari were going to open an art scholarship in Kat's name, and they both thanked Wilma profusely for solving the case. Both were still in mourning over Kat and the lost years of friendship, but Wilma hoped that they would get some comfort knowing that they might have reconciled with a little more time.

"If only the mystery of the chocolate egg was as easily solved,"

Wilma said that night. Jason had joined her at her cabin for a meal, and would be taking part in a few of the last art classes the following day. "Do you have any leads on who stole it?"

"Nothing solid," Jason answered. "I have a suspect in mind."

Wilma's eyes widened. "One of the other officers in the precinct?"'

Jason shook his head. "It's best if I don't tell you. But I'm not giving up, Wilma. We'll figure this out. I promise."

"Thank you." Wilma reached into her pocket and produced two identical friendship bracelets. She handed one to Jason. "Here. I made this for you. I made a matching pair for me and my cousin, but then I thought I'd make another set."

Jason grinned. "Miss Wade, I'm touched."

Wilma laughed. "You better be. It took me forever to get that foundation bead in place!"

The End

MURDER AT THE PARTY

A SMALL-TOWN HALLOWEEN COZY
MYSTERY WITH A SENIOR SLEUTH

CHAPTER ONE

"AHH, Agatha Christie. You look very much like a writer friend of mine," Detective Jason Fellow said, bowing slightly to an elegantly dressed woman who stood on Wilma Wade's porch. She wore a red wool suit and a pair of beaded necklaces, with her hair styled just so.

Wilma Wade laughed at Detective Fellow's joke and shook her head. "Now, now, Detective. Don't start getting smart with me."

Jason smirked and offered her his arm. "Careful, your sidewalk is a little slippery."

"Oh, dear." Wilma groaned. "Don't tell me we're getting ice already. It's barely the end of October!"

"It's almost the beginning of November," Jason corrected as they started toward his car. He wore a checkered cloak and a deer-stalker hat. Maybe it was a bit on the nose for a detective to dress up as Sherlock Holmes, but he said it was just a fun little nod to his profession.

The trees were nearly all bare and there was a nip of frost in the air. Wilma breathed in deeply, enjoying the taste of Halloween night.

"You did a great job on these costumes," Jason said as they got to his car. He opened the door for her.

Wilma blushed and slid inside. She waited until Jason had gotten in on his side before she said, "Well, they did turn out alright. I'm not the best seamstress."

Jason wagged at finger at her. "You need to stop being so self-deprecating. You're always saying you're not the best baker, not the best seamstress, not the best writer. You've got a lot of talent and skills, Miss Wade. Even if you aren't a master at everything, you're still a jack-of-all-trades and you should acknowledge that you're good at what you do."

"Oh, you!" Wilma shook her head, blushing but pleased with Jason's words. He really was a sweet boy. Wilma had never been blessed with a child herself, but if she had she would hope that she'd have a son like Jason Fellow.

"If you weren't good at what you do, the mayor wouldn't have asked for you to read one of your short stories at the party," Jason added.

Wilma clutched at her seatbelt, groaning. "Alright, alright. It appears that I'm not half-bad. Is it my fault that I'm uncomfortable with all the praise and people talking to me about myself? It's so dreadfully..."

"Public?" Jason suggested.

"I was always taught that I should be demure and not get too big of a head," Wilma answered. "It's strange stepping into the spotlight after a lifetime of nondescription."

"It's a spotlight that you deserve, Miss Wade. And I'd bet if we asked your old students, more than one of them would describe you as something other than nondescript."

Wilma laughed, touched at his encouragement.

Tonight was the Barwick Halloween Costume Party at the community center. It had been planned by the mayor as a way to encourage community engagement. While all costumes were welcome, there was a particular contest that was directed at the best costume related to mysteries. Wilma had decided that since she was going to be doing a reading, she might as well dress up as the Queen of Crime herself.

They reached the community center quickly. It was decorated with cobwebs, jack-o'-lanterns, and outdoor haybales, with orange, black and purple ribbons twisting in great snakes over the room. The lighting was just dim enough to be spooky, but still bright enough that nobody ran the risk of getting hurt. Wilma laughed in delight when she saw it all.

"It looks like a gothic castle," she told Jason.

"Oh, and there's the refreshment table," he said, pointing. There was a long, low table at the back where servers were handing out drinks and small snacks.

They stepped out of the entrance and took a moment to look around. Wilma eyed various guests and took a moment to figure out who they might be. She found Miss Marple, Jessica Fletcher, Columbo, James Moriarty, and someone she thought was Nancy Drew. It was all very delightful. Clearly, lots of people had put a great deal of thought and effort into their costumes.

Wilma drank in the atmosphere, her fingers itching to write down every sensation she was having. She had been thinking for a while now she wanted to write a Halloween-themed mystery, and this party seemed to be just the place to start. Of course, rather than a community center, she would have a real gothic castle. Instead of streamers, she'd have chandeliers. Maybe a few ghouls or goblins as well...

"Oh, there's the commissioner," Jason said, gesturing to someone dressed as Captain Kidd. "I had best go say hello. Do you want to go with me?"

"I'll make my way to him later. Right now, I just want to memorize everything that's in my mind's eye," she answered.

Jason moved off and Wilma moved to the wall so she could observe everything even better. A tall guest wearing a fearsome devil mask caught her eye. She watched him, fascinated. The mask was very detailed and seemed expertly crafted. He wore a hooded cloak so she couldn't see how it was connected, but it almost looked as though he's put a helmet on. What sort of material was it, anyway?

With these questions bubbling up, Wilma headed over to him. He moved in slow circles, his head swinging back and forth as though he was looking for something.

"Hello, there," Wilma greeted as she stepped in front of him. "That is a terrific costume you have."

"Thanks," the man answered.

"Did you make your mask or did you buy it?" she asked.

The man looked up her up and down. "Made it."

"You have a lot of talent. What did you use—"

"Excuse me," he grunted and brushed past her.

Wilma watched him go, a little startled. But then it did look like he was searching for someone. Maybe he just didn't want to take the time to talk with a stranger? There was something about the interaction that left Wilma unsettled, but she tried to brush it off as being due to the spooky atmosphere. She watched the masked man for a while. He didn't stop to talk anyone, continually moving through the crowd.

She spied Suzanne Wilkins, one of the local farmers and moved over to her side. "Suzanne, you look amazing! You are Brennan Temperance, right?"

Suzanne beamed. "Of course!"

"Have you seen that tall masked man?" Wilma asked. "Do you know who he is?"

"I saw him, yes, but I don't know who he is." Suzanne shivered. "He looks pretty scary, doesn't he? It's an amazing costume."

"It really is." Wilma frowned as she watched the masked man.

He'd stopped, his head turning. When he started walking again, it was with wide strides that seemed fiercely determined. Wilma searched the crowd ahead of him and caught the sight of a blonde wig. Was that Nancy Drew? She seemed to be running away from him. Wilma's heart jumped to her throat and she hurried forward, pushing through the crowd. She's seen Nancy Drew earlier and she was only a young girl—why would she be running away from the masked man? Was he dangerous?

Unfortunately, after only a few steps Miss Marple accidentally bumped into her. Wilma pitched to the side, losing her balance.

"Oh, I'm so sorry!" Miss Marple helped her back to her feet. "I didn't see you. Are you alright, Miss Wade?"

"I am, thank you," Wilma said distractedly. She searched the crowd, but neither the masked man nor Nancy Drew were in sight anymore. Worry ate at her stomach as she hurried off again. She saw no sign of either of them, but soon made her way to Detective Fellow. She told him about what she had seen. "I'm worried that he might be trying to hurt her."

Jason looked serious as he searched the crowd. "Ah! There's Nancy Drew," he said, pointing.

Sure enough, the blonde wig was back in the crowd. She was behind the refreshment table now, standing with the other volunteers. Though her expression seemed stressed, she wasn't so frightened. Wilma soon saw the masked man again, at the opposite side of the center. She relaxed a little.

"I'll keep an eye on him, if you want to go talk with Nancy and see what's wrong," Jason suggested, squinting.

Wilma nodded in gratitude. She could always count on Jason to have her back. She moved off again, heading for the refreshment table. As she approached, Nancy Drew kept looking over at the masked man. When Wilma glanced over her shoulder again, she saw that he had started to approach the refreshment table, too. Jason intervened, stepping in front of the man.

Good! Maybe Wilma would be able to get some answers to this very suspicious behavior. She turned back around only to find that Nancy was no longer near the refreshments table. She looked around wildly and saw the blonde wig disappearing into the women's bathroom.

Quickly, Wilma made her way over there. The door was a little sticky but she managed to shove it open. As soon as she did, she shivered as a blast of cold air wafted to her. She let the door swing shut as she looked around. All the stalls were open and empty... but there, at the back of the bathroom, was a window. It had been opened.

Wilma hurried to it and peered outside. A car was driving away from the parking lot. And lying on the ground just below the window was a blonde wig.

CHAPTER TWO

WAS Nancy Drew running from the man because she was in danger?

Worried, Wilma went back to the party. She quickly spotted the masked guest again and relaxed. So even if Nancy Drew was avoiding him, at least he wasn't chasing her. Detective Fellow was still talking with the man, so Wilma left him to it. Maybe he'd have better luck at deciphering what happened than she had.

She went back to the refreshment table, where Nancy Drew had been. There, she smiled at the volunteers. "Excuse me, can you tell me who that young woman who had been over here is? I can't find her anywhere and I wanted to tell her what an excellent costume she has."

The volunteer looked around, frowning. "Hmm. That's strange, she was right here. I'm sure she'll be back later; she was very excited about the mystery costume contest. Her name is Nancy Brustatte and she is just the sweetest girl."

"Thank you so much," Wilma said.

By this time, Jason was no longer talking with the masked man. Wilma met his eye and nodded outside. They slipped out of the community center into the cool October night. There, Wilma told Jason what she had found out. Though he'd spoken with the masked man, he hadn't learned anything about him.

"I'm still concerned for Nancy," Wilma said.

Jason pulled out his phone. "Let's give her a call. Brustatte is in the phonebook, with any luck that's her."

He dialed a number and a young woman's voice answered. "Hello?"

"Hello. Is this Nancy Brustatte?" he said.

"Yes, it is. Who's this?" Nancy asked.

Jason nodded. "I'm Detective Jason Fellow. A witness saw you fleeing through the window in the community center and was concerned for you. Are you alright?"

"What?" Nancy laughed nervously. "Of course I am. I'm fine. Perfectly fine."

"Miss Brustatte, if there's anything the department can do for you, please don't hesitate to call."

Nancy sighed. "Thank you, Detective. The truth is, I did run away through the bathroom window. But it's just a stupid prank someone pulled on me. Nothing is worth getting the police involved. I'm sorry for wasting your time, Detective. In fact, I'm heading back to the party right now."

Wilma and Jason looked at each other as Nancy hung up.

"I'm going to wait out here for her to return," Wilma said, her eyebrows pinched. "Why don't you go back inside, Jason? No use in us both freezing our tails off."

Jason put a hand on her arm. "You don't know when she'll be coming back. Let's both go back inside."

Wilma let Jason lead her back inside. She tried to get into the party but kept looking out for the young woman. It was only fifteen minutes later that she showed up. By this time, the masked man had disappeared, and Wilma was happy for it. She made her way to Nancy, who seemed to recognize her as the concerned party that had Jason call her.

"Miss Wade, I'm fine. Thank you so much for your concern," Nancy said, squeezing Wilma's hand. "I appreciate you looking out for me. The truth is, I thought that the man in the mask was my stepfather."

"Oh?" Wilma said, surprised.

Nancy shook her head. "You see, five years ago I was working at a gas station when it was robbed. It was my stepfather. I recognized a tattoo he had on his arm of a snake. He was always into all this crazy occult stuff and had tried to make me get that tattoo, too. He said it would ward off the curse that ran in his blood. I refused and he just got angrier and angrier."

"That sounds scary," Wilma said sympathetically.

"It was. Eventually, I convinced my mom to leave him. That night at the gas station, I'm certain he was hoping that somehow it would convince me that this curse he was always going on about was real." Nancy shuddered. "Anyway, with my testimony, he was convicted of that robbery and several others. Ten years in jail. I thought that somehow that man was him. But I called the lawyer that handled his case and she assured me that he was still in jail. So, it was just my overactive imagination."

Wilma nodded her understanding. "It must have been terrifying."

"It was. But it's over now," Nancy said. "And it's time for the costume contest. Are you participating?"

Wilma smiled at Nancy and nodded. "Let's head over, shall we?"

They made their way to the front of the hall, where others wearing their mystery costumes also gathered around. Wilma's heart fluttered with nerves. Right after this contest, she would be reading her short story, like the mayor asked. She smoothed a hand over her jacket, feeling the papers that her story was written on. Though Wilma was very comfortable reading her stories at places like the hospital and the senior's center, this was a whole other ball game.

Just as the mayor started to tap the microphone, a scream suddenly rang through the hall. Nancy tensed and Wilma quickly searched for Jason. He was already making his way toward the sound and Wilma hurried to join him. The crowd murmured and swayed like a giant, living organism, moving forward and back. Finally, Wilma pushed through. Miss Marple stood over the masked man, who was crumpled in a heap on the dance floor.

A dagger protruded from his ribs.

"You, call 9-1-1," Jason said, pointing at a man dressed as Moriarty.

Wilma peered closer at the man on the floor. His costume was soaked with blood. She shivered. This was no staged act. She pressed a hand to her heart, her throat dry. A murder in the middle of a party? Who did it? How could they have pulled it off?

"Everyone back away," Jason said, slipping into Detective mode. He took off her deerstalker hat and Sherlock Holmes coat. He knelt beside the masked man and first tried to take off the mask, but it wouldn't budge, so he checked for a pulse. He shook his head sadly.

Anyone could be the killer. Wilma gazed at the crowd, trying to analyze everyone she was seeing. Nobody had any visible blood on them. But surely the killer would have fled the scene immediately?

"He's dead." Jason stood and frowned. "Wilma, can you take over the call for 9-1-1? Mr. Moriarty, please help me move the victim to the supply closet."

He looked around at the crowd, his gaze sharp. Wilma understood. With so many people here, the crime scene was pretty much useless. It was best to get the body away from these prying eyes. Wilma took the phone and explained to the operator what was going on; they would be sending more police over right away to help Jason take people's statements and to process what they could.

As Jason and Moriarty lifted the body, Wilma frowned. Despite the masked man's costume being soaked in blood, there was no trace of any on the floor. Odd. With that much blood, there should be puddles of it left behind, but there wasn't even a smudge.

Wilma followed the detective as he carried the body to the storage closet. Once there, Moriarty took back his phone and quickly left. Jason pulled on a pair of latex gloves.

"I don't have a pair for you," he said to Wilma apologetically. "And I don't have any evidence bags."

Wilma produced one from her pocket. "I always carry one with me these days. I've ended up involved in too many murder cases."

Jason sighed. "And it looks like we have another mystery on our hands."

"There was no blood on the floor," Wilma said.

Jason nodded. "I noticed that, too. Let's get the mask off him and see if we can identify him." He reached for the mask again but frowned. After a moment, he whistled. "I don't get it. It's like the mask has been welded in place. I can't find any latches on it at all."

"Check his arms," Wilma suggested. "If he has a snake tattoo, I think I might know who it is."

Jason pulled up the man's sleeves. There was no tattoo. Wilma frowned as she knelt, peering closer.

"Well, there's that theory gone," she sighed.

She studied the mask, trying to get a glimpse of the face behind it. She squinted and a chill stole down her spine. "Jason, look. You can see through the mouth a little into his mouth. Are those… vampire fangs?"

Jason pulled out a flashlight and shone it into the mask. Sure enough, two long white fangs glinted under the light. Even as poor a view as they had, Wilma knew instantly that those weren't a fake plastic set. She met Jason's eye and they both stared at each other.

"It must be a high-end costume," Jason muttered.

"What do you mean?"

Jason shook his head. "I mean those are quality veneers. Must have cost a pretty penny."

He started to search the man's clothes while Wilma inspected the dagger. They hadn't removed it—hopefully there would be prints on it—but Wilma could still see that it was made out of silver. A silver dagger and vampire fangs? She frowned. Wasn't silver just used against werewolves? Someone seemed to be getting their paranormal myths mixed up.

"There's a note in his pocket," Jason said, pulling out a piece of paper. He frowned at it as he shook his head. "Blood to vengeance. You will feel my wrath."

"Oooh." Wilma shuddered. "Do you think the killer slipped him the note? Or was he planning on slipping it to someone else?"

Wilma thought about Nancy. She had been standing right next to Wilma when the masked man was killed. But what if… "Jason, can you check his arms again? Look for any sign that a tattoo might be removed or covered up."

Jason checked the arms again. He paused when he came to a slightly discolored patch. "Look here. It looks like there might be makeup on his arm hairs. If I…" He carefully rubbed at the spot. Foundation came off, revealing the head of a snake.

"Oh, dear." Wilma wrapped her arms around herself. "I think I know who this is. But the question is, how is he here? He's supposed to be in jail."

CHAPTER THREE

"WHO IS IT?" Jason asked, his brow furrowing.

Wilma quickly explained what Nancy Brustatte had told her about her stepfather. Jason grew more serious as he straightened. The sound of the other police officers arriving at the party had made its way to them. Wilma knew they didn't have much time. The sight of the dead man and all the police would no doubt terrify Nancy.

"He must have covered up the snake so she wouldn't see who he was," Wilma said. "And this note... it might have been meant for her."

"Find Nancy and see if you can get the lawyer's number," Jason told her, looking grim. "I'll send someone to look up the file while I process the body and see if I can get a witness to come forward. Oh, and that Miss Marple was very close to the body. If you see her, send her in my direction, okay?"

Wilma nodded, determined. How could a murder happen in the middle of a party... and how could a body covered in blood leave no blood on the floor? What was Nancy's stepfather doing here? Why was Nancy convinced he was in jail if he was here in Barwick?

There were so many questions to be answered, and Wilma couldn't help but feel a certain sense of responsibility. She had noticed Nancy afraid of the masked man, but had talked herself out of her instincts.

She looked around, trying to find Nancy or Miss Marple, but even though the lights were on bright now, she saw no sign of either of them. The crowd seemed to be thinner now. Oh dear. It looked like witnesses had decided to leave the hall. While she understood that most of them would think that they couldn't actually share anything of importance, it would have been nice for them to stay and wait for the police to tell them what to do.

When Wilma spotted the mayor, she went for him. He was speaking with a few of the others, trying to placate them.

"I'm sure it was just an accident," he was saying.

"Mr. Mayor," Wilma called. "I need you to make an announcement. We need everyone to stay calm and stay here until the police can get their statements. Please, before anyone else leaves," she added, noting another party heading for the door.

The mayor looked flustered. "Of course, Miss Wade."

As he went to the microphone and made the announcement, Wilma hurried outside. The police were, thankfully, directing foot traffic back into the building, although several arguments were happening. Wilma hurried toward the cars and a young officer caught her eye and frowned.

"Ma'am, we're asking everyone to—" he started, then stopped. "Oh, it's you, Miss Wade. Did Detective Fellow send you for something?"

"Yes, he did. I won't be but a minute," Wilma promised. She hurried toward the cars, shaking her head when there was a chorus of "But she can go through!" from behind her. She searched the parking lot for any sign of Nancy or Miss Marple. There was nothing, but maybe they had already gotten into their cars and were just hiding out until the police let everyone leave.

Wilma headed back to the young officer who had stopped her

before. "Officer, I think you should walk through the parking lot and see if anyone is hiding in their cars. I would do it myself but I'm afraid that seeing a civilian wandering will make the others restless," she added, nodding toward the guests who were reluctantly turning back to the community center.

"Thank you, Miss Wade," the officer said. "I will get right on that. In the meantime, could you go back inside as well? It's just... well, like you said the others are getting restless."

Wilma nodded her understanding.

She headed back inside and smiled when she saw that Miss Marple had gone back inside as well. She lingered in a small knot of ladies Wilma's age, as though she was trying to hide from the police. She watched them with an anxious expression as she shrank back against the refreshment table.

Wilma made her way over to the knot of ladies, which included someone dressed as Jessica Fletcher from *Murder, She Wrote* and another as someone Wilma suspected was Emily Pollifax from *The Unexpected Mrs. Pollifax.*

"This has been quite the awful turn of events, hasn't it?" Wilma said as she stepped up to the group. "I don't think we've met before. I'm Wilma Wade."

"Billie Marks," Jessica Fletcher said. "And this is my sister, Jenny Kephart."

Wilma shook their hands smiling. "And you are?" she asked Miss Marple.

"Margaret Lowell," the woman answered coolly. She wrapped her arms around herself and peered at Wilma with undisguised suspicion. "You're that retired teacher that works with the police, aren't you? The one that solved that llama murder a few months back."

Billie's eyes widened. "Oh, was that you? I read about it in the newspaper. All those exotic animals rescued. You must be very proud of yourself."

"I am, thank you." Wilma nodded, smiling. "I noticed that

Margaret was nearby when that poor man was... well, I'm not sure exactly what happened. Did you see anything?"

Margaret shook her head. "I was talking with that man dressed as Moriarty—"

"That would be my husband," Billie put in. "Vincent."

"Oh. Well, I was talking to Vincent," Margaret said with a small shrug. "There was this young lady in a blonde wig that pushed by me and when I turned to see if she needed anything, that's when that man collapsed. It all happened so fast. I don't understand what happened. One moment everything was fine, then he was on the floor. I screamed, naturally. The girl disappeared into the crowd and I thought I saw her heading for the exit."

A second young woman in a blonde wig? Could it be that the one Wilma had seen sneak out of the bathroom wasn't Nancy at all? When she returned, she had her wig again... but no, Nancy herself admitted she had climbed out of the window. So, what could it be?

"I saw a young woman in a blonde wig," Jenny said. She put her hands on her hips. "She was over near the refreshments table earlier today."

Wilma shook her head. "Oh, it can't be the same young woman. The one dressed as Nancy Drew?"

Jenny nodded.

"I was standing with her over on the other side of the hall when the man collapsed," Wilma explained. "So, it can't have been her. We must be looking for another young woman. Can you tell me anything else about her?"

Margaret pursed her lips and shook her head slowly. "No. I'm sorry, I didn't get a good glimpse of her."'

As they spoke, a man dressed as Nero Wolfe made his way to the refreshments table. He ladled himself a glass of punch, shaking his head and muttering. He looked rather uncomfortable and Wilma frowned at him. She could swear that she'd seen him nearby when she and Jason got to the body on the floor. Just as she was about to excuse herself from the ladies and speak with him, he swayed on the spot. He keeled over, collapsing to the floor.

"Medic," Wilma shouted, pushing past the three ladies to drop to her knees beside the man. She checked his breathing and his pulse. Both were steady.

The paramedics got to her quickly, but by that time, Nero was already coming around. He sat up, his eyes bleary and confused. "Huh? What happened?"

Wilma let out a sigh of relief. She got out of the way of the paramedics as Jason joined her. She explained what happened and turned to the punch bowl.

"Does it have a strange scent to you?" she asked, sniffing at the ladle.

Jason took it, smelled the punch, and nodded. "It doesn't smell normal. My guess is that it's been spiked. I'll have a sample taken to be analyzed. Do you think that whoever stabbed the masked man also spiked the punch?"

Wilma tapped her chin thoughtfully. "It might be. Having something else to take the police's attention might have allowed someone to slip out. Have you seen Nancy?"

"No. None of the officers have seen her," Jason answered.

"Are there any other young women wearing blonde wigs?"

Jason shook his head. "No. Why?"

Wilma hummed in thought. "One of the witnesses saw a young woman wearing a blonde wig near the victim just before he collapsed. Oh!" She pointed across the hall to where a blonde wig bounced toward the door. "Jason, look!"

The Detective hurried through the crowd. The paramedics helped Nero to his feet and started to walk him outside to take him to the hospital while one of the other police officers took a sample of the punch. Everything seemed to happen all at once, distracting Wilma. By the time she looked back at Jason, he was standing next to the doors, frowning. The blonde wig was nowhere to be seen.

CHAPTER FOUR

WILMA MADE her way to Jason, who stood near the doors talking with the police officers stationed there. They all looked confused. Jason ran a hand through his hair, catching Wilma's eye as she approached. A frown furrowed between his brows and his jaw was tight. Oh, dear. That didn't look good at all. She looked around, but found no sign of the blonde wig.

"No, Sir, nobody of that description passed through," the young officer said, shaking his head.

"Then where did she go?" Jason muttered, running his hand through his hair again. "Wilma, have you seen Nancy at all?"

Wilma shook her head.

The paramedics took Nero out and the crowd pressed around, demanding that Jason let them all go home. Wilma shared a look with the Detective, stepping back to observe the crowd while he tried to keep them calm. There was no sign of Nancy or a blonde wig anywhere. How had she disappeared so easily?

She thought about the legends of vampires, how they were able to turn into bats or cats or other creatures and slip away unseen. A shiver ran down Wilma's spine. Vampires weren't real! And if they were, then the murder victim was the vampire, not Nancy. She just wished she knew what the man's name was! So far, she didn't even have that much information. How were they meant to solve the mystery if they didn't have even the most basic information?

A hand tugged her sleeve. She turned but there was nobody there. The chills increased and she gasped, catching sight of a glimpse of a blonde wig near the bathrooms. She grabbed Jason's arm and towed him along, not bothering to be polite as she pushed through the crowd. The door to the men's bathroom opened and the blonde wig disappeared again.

They reached the bathroom quickly. Jason entered, Wilma hesitating just a moment at the doorway before she entered as well. Normally, there wasn't anything that would compel her to enter the men's washroom, but this was an emergency. There was no place for modesty when it came to murder investigations.

Fortunately, it was empty except Vincent Marks, dressed as Moriarty, scrubbing at a bloodstain on the sleeve of his shirt. He jumped, his face going pale when he saw the two of them enter the washroom.

"Oh, Detective. What are you, um, what are you doing here?" he asked, a sheen of sweat glistening on his forehead as he gave a weak smile.

"Did someone else come into the bathroom just now?" Jason asked, looking around with a frustrated expression.

Vincent straightened. "No. I mean, the door opened just before you came in but nobody was there. Why? Are you looking for someone?"

"There was a person with a blonde wig that came to the bathroom door and then disappeared into the crowd," Jason answered. He shook his head as his eyes met Wilma's. Nancy had used a bathroom to escape before. Had she thought she was going to the women's bathroom, only to see Vincent?

Wilma stepped forward and pointed at Vincent's bloody sleeve. "How did that happen?"

"Oh, this." Vincent glanced nervously toward the door behind them. "It must have happened when I helped move the body. I just noticed it and I thought I had best get it off before someone got the wrong idea. You know, since I had been standing right there when that man was stabbed."

He shuddered, looking at the door again. It opened, making him jump. Wilma turned to see Margaret step in. Her brows were pinched together and she fidgeted, smoothing her hands down over her skirt.

"I'm so sorry to interrupt, but I thought I might be able to be of some help. I was speaking with Vincent just before the man collapsed. We were close to him but Vincent wasn't close enough to have stabbed anyone," Margaret insisted. "It was that young girl in the wig, I'm sure of it. I thought I saw her again just a moment ago but she disappeared into the crowd."

Vincent nodded, the sweat glistening brighter on his face. Wilma frowned at him. If that was the truth, why was he so nervous? Unless... unless his sweating wasn't because of nerves at all?

"Did you drink any of the punch?" she asked him.

"What? Yes," Vincent said. He lifted a glass sitting on the bathroom sink. "I have some right here."

Jason let out a huffed breath. "Mr. Marks, I need you to sit down right now. The punch was spiked. Wilma, please get the paramedics in here right away."

Margaret followed Wilma out. "Miss Wade—"

"In a moment, please," Wilma said.

She identified one of the paramedics still here and hurried over to her. After explaining what happened, Wilma sought out the mayor and had him make an announcement for everyone who still had punch to give it to the police and report if they had any sort of symptoms to the paramedics. The reasons for spiking the punch seemed to be more obvious than ever. The killer was hoping to keep the police in a state of panic and constantly putting out fires, letting them contaminate the scene further.

As Vincent Marks was being taken to the ambulance, several others got sick as well. Wilma was worried about whether the killer was faking symptoms to get out of the hall, but there was no telling who was really sick and who wasn't. The police took the information of everyone as they were taken to the hospital. By this time, the crowd was quite anxious, with many of them trying to leave before they could be targeted.

"This isn't going to be as simple as it seems," Jason told Wilma. He shook his head warily. "I think we have to let them go. We aren't going to be able to find out anything if everyone is in such a state of panic."

Wilma had to agree. "I haven't seen anything of Nancy. I think it's time that we gave her a call. She might have fled the scene because of her previous encounter with the masked man."

"You were standing right next to her. That's an alibi if ever there was one," Jason pointed out.

"People don't always think things through when they're frightened," Wilma answered. She pulled out her phone and started to look for a quiet place where she might be able to make the call.

Maragret stepped in front of her. "Miss Wade, I hate to be a bother, but I found something that you might need to see."

She pressed a piece of paper in Wilma's hand. Wilma glanced at it and opened her mouth to ask where she'd gotten it, but Margaret melted into the passage of the guests as they streamed out of the hall. She quickly lost sight of the other woman. Among the crowd, she thought she saw a blonde wig but when she blinked, it was just silver hair.

Wilma looked at the paper. A message was scrawled over it in the same writing as the note they had found on the masked man's body.

He will rise again.

Wilma shuddered and shoved the note into her pocket. She

quickly called Nancy's number. There was no answer. She tried again to the same result.

Quickly, she sought out Jason. He was talking with some of the other police, directing them, but turned to Wilma when she tapped his shoulder. Once seeing her expression, he straightened.

"I'm worried about Nancy. She's not answering her phone," Wilma said. "Would you be kind enough to find her address so we can go check on her?"

"Of course," Jason said readily. He took care of the rest of what he needed to do here at the community hall, then he and Wilma headed out. As they drove, Wilma shared with him the note that Margaret had handed her.

Wilma slumped into her seat when she was done. "I have to say, Margaret's behavior is rather suspicious. But she was talking to Vincent when the man was stabbed, so I don't know what part in all of this she could have."

"She could have put something in the punch. The real question is why?" Jason shook his head as he pulled into a driveway. "I'll have my people look into her. Maybe there's a connection between her and the victim." He turned off the cruiser. "The lights are on. That's a good sign."

They got out of the car and headed up the driveway. Just as they were almost to the door, it opened. Nancy stood haloed in the lighting, her shoulders slumped.

"Detective Fellow. Miss Wade. Please come in," she said.

Wilma sighed in relief. "You gave us quite a fright, young lady," she said sternly. "I was so worried for you when I couldn't find you."

Nancy winced. She led them to the living room. It was a lovely room with dark furniture and a white rug on the hardwood floor. She sank into a chair and settled her head into her hands. "I know, and I'm sorry. It only occurred to me about five minutes ago that I shouldn't have taken off. I was just so frightened when that man was stabbed. That knife... it looked exactly the same as the knife my stepfather used to rob the gas station."

Wilma and Jason glanced at each other.

"Who was the lawyer in charge of the case?" Wilma asked gently.

Nancy frowned. "Oh, um, I never actually met her. My stepfather pled guilty, you see, so there wasn't actually a trial. Her name was Maggie. I don't know her last name. Why?"

"We have reason to believe you may have been right, and that was your stepfather." Jason showed her a picture of the tattoo on the man's arm. "Is that your stepfather's tattoo?"

Nancy gasped. "It is. What does this mean? Maggie said he was in jail! How could he be at the party?"

CHAPTER FIVE

"HOW, INDEED?" Wilma rubbed her forehead. It was getting so late and she was tired. Her mind wasn't quite as sharp as it could be. "Nancy, what is your stepfather's name?"

Nancy wrinkled her nose. "Douglas Creel."

Wilma frowned. That name was familiar. "Yes, I remember reading about his case in the papers. It was all very quick, wasn't it? It seemed like it was going to be one of those long, drawn-out things but it suddenly went away when he plead guilty. Do you know why he decided to do that?"

"No. I'm sorry. I'm not sure what help I can be. I thought it was him at first but then Maggie assured me he was still in jail... how could it be him?" Nancy twisted her hands together.

"I'll need the lawyer's number," Jason said.

Nancy nodded and pulled out her phone. "Of course."

Wilma ran her hand through her hair as she listened to the number being read aloud. Afterward, Jason told Nancy to call them if she thought of anything or felt as though she was in danger. They were both quiet as they went back to the car.

"Maggie..." Wilma murmured. "Do you think Margaret could be involved in this?"

If she was the one that Nancy called, then she knew that Nancy's stepfather was out of jail and lured her back to the party. Then, when she said she saw a young woman in a blonde wig... Hmmm. There were all these pieces but they weren't quite forming a puzzle.

"I'm not sure. We have to keep in mind the possibility that Nancy was lying about calling his lawyer," Jason said. "It's possible that she set some sort of trap for him. But we still don't know where the killing took place."

Wilma sighed. "I don't think I'll be of much good anymore tonight, Detective. Can you take me home? I'll be up bright and early tomorrow to tackle the problem with fresh eyes."

In the morning, Wilma drove herself to the precinct. There, she met with Jason, who revealed that the morgue had managed to get the mask off their masked man and ran his fingerprints. Their murder victim was, in fact, Douglas Creel. The only fingerprints on the silver dagger were his own.

"He escaped from prison sometime yesterday, but it wasn't discovered that he was missing until this morning," Jason told Wilma.

"So then 'Maggie' wouldn't have known that Douglas had escaped when Nancy called her. Did you verify that it was Margaret Lowell?" Wilma asked.

"I did. She claims that she didn't know that Nancy lived here in Barwick. They hadn't talked since Douglas decided to plead guilty. There was no need for it," Jason said. He handed Wilma a folder file. "This is the ME's report about their findings on Douglas. It gets stranger. The blood soaking his costume is pig's blood. When they removed the dagger from his body, it was clean and dry. There's no blood on his body, either."

Wilma's eyes widened. "What do you mean?"

"His throat was cut and his body drained," Jason answered. "Then he was stabbed and brought back to the party. The entire thing seems as though it was staged, but for what reason? That's what I can't figure out. Those vampire fangs you saw through the mask also turned out to be real. His teeth had grown and shaped themselves like that."

"Jason..." Wilma wrapped her arms around herself. "You don't think... I mean, it's not possible that he was really a... a vampire?"

Jason frowned at her but didn't laugh. "If he was a vampire, then what would his motive be to come to the party? It seemed as though he was seeking out Nancy, but why would he do that rather than go to her house and exact his revenge there?"

"Maybe he was after Margaret as well?" Wilma suggested.

She knew that what she was saying was rather silly. After all, vampires weren't real. Even if they were, a vampire wouldn't be killed by getting their throat cut. No, this had a fully rational explanation. It had to have.

"Maybe we're looking at this wrong," she murmured. "Jason, you said the body had no blood in it. That had to take time, but the masked man was missing from the party for only a short time. What if the man we saw walking around wasn't Douglas Creel? What if he was already dead, and the man we saw was an imposter?"

Jason nodded, frowning. "That's a good idea. The only question is, how are we going to find him? We have no leads as to who else might be involved in this."

Wilma frowned. "Jason... does Douglas Creel have any family?"

"He has a brother. Why? Do you think his brother killed him and staged this?" Jason asked, frowning.

"I don't know. But I do know that this means Nancy might be in danger still." Wilma jumped to her feet. "We need to go check on her at once!"

They rushed out of the station. Wilma's heart slammed into her chest as they headed to Nancy's home on the outskirts of town. The clear November day was crisp, with the colorful leaves rustling on the trees. Wilma drummed her fingers impatiently on the car door. They arrived at Nancy's house to see an unfamiliar car parked in the driveway and the door ajar.

Wilma's heart sank as they came to a stop.

"Stay in the car," Jason ordered as he hopped out. He drew his service weapon as he headed for the door.

Wilma tried to obey. She really did. It was dangerous and she didn't want to make it even more dangerous. But when Jason disappeared in the house, she unbuckled her seatbelt and stepped out of the car. She gripped the door tightly, peering toward the house and straining her ears. After several long minutes, the radio in the car made a noise.

"Wilma, you can come in," Jason said over the radio.

Quickly, she headed inside. As she passed through the door, she saw that the frame had been splintered, as though someone had taken a crowbar to it. Her heart skipped a beat and she rushed in, calling out for Jason.

"In here," Jason answered.

Wilma hurried into the living room. There, the once-pristine white carpet was stained with blood pooling around a body. Wilma gasped but as she drew nearer, she saw that it wasn't what she feared. It wasn't Nancy's body at all. Nancy was sitting on a chair, her knees drawn up to her chest, her eyes wide and red from crying.

"Who is it?" Wilma asked, her voice hushed.

Jason shook his head. "Richard Creel. Douglas's brother."

"I heard a noise," Nancy whispered. "I heard a noise and came looking. He was already dead on the floor. I tried to call the cops but my phone didn't work. Then... then I just couldn't move. It was

MURDER AT THE PARTY

like I was frozen. I could only just stand there and stare at the body until the Detective came in."

Wilma approached the body. With this amount of blood, she expected to see a visible wound. But all she could see on him were two perfectly clean holes in his neck, set apart just right to be vampire teeth.

———

"The blood on the carpet belongs to Douglas Creel," Jason told her some time later. "Richard was killed by a massive overdose of morphine. Those holes that looked like bite marks were made post-mortem. My guess is that Richard was in on Douglas's death and whoever his partner is killed him, too."

"The question is, why?" Wilma shook her head slowly. "I can understand leaving the body and blood at Nancy's house. They were trying to frame her. But what I can't understand is why they decided to kill the Creel brothers at all. It's all just so confusing."

She cupped her chin in her hand, running over the events of the night. Clearly, the entire thing was meant to cause Nancy emotional distress and try to paint her as a killer. Who could have such a vendetta against her, though?

"I think we need to talk to Margaret," Wilma said, lifting her head. "She's the only other person in town who is connected to both Nancy and Douglas Creel. Maybe she is also involved in the death somehow."

Jason nodded.

They drove to Margaret's B&B rental. The car parked outside was pristine and sparkled as though it was freshly cleaned. Jason knocked on the front door to no answer, so Wilma went around the side, peering over a low hedge into the backyard.

She gasped.

"Jason!" she called.

A body lay on the ground. Silver hair spilled around Margaret

Lowell's head as what looked like a wooden stake speared straight through her body. Wilma's hands shook—until Margaret opened her eyes.

"What?" she said pushing herself to a sitting position. "Who's there?"

CHAPTER SIX

JASON AND WILMA entered the backyard, both of them frowning. Wilma hurried over to see that the stake had been stabbed into the ground beside Margaret. She sighed in relief. That had been a close one! She turned to Margaret with a puzzled frown.

"What are you doing, laying on the ground like that?" she asked. "I'm your age and there's no way I'd willingly lay around on the cold, hard ground."

Margaret got stiffly to her feet. She was still wearing her Miss Marple outfit from the party last night. "I was attacked. There was a man wearing a long cape. He bit my neck and I tried to fight back with this stake but he disappeared."

"Where did he bite you?" Jason asked in concern.

As Margaret showed him, Wilma frowned at the spot of earth that the stake had been driven into. That hardly seemed like an accident. If anything, there was something decidedly odd about how deliberate it seemed. It seemed as though that spot had been dug up. But why? As Margaret was describing the attack, Wilma nudged the pile of earth with her toe.

Something was buried here. She looked up quickly, making sure

Margaret was still engrossed, then stooped. As she did so, Margaret's head spun toward her.

"What are you doing?" Margaret cried, jumping forward.

It was too late. Wilma straightened, holding a blonde wig covered in dirt. It was styled in the same way as Nancy's had been from the previous night. Wilma turned to Margaret, lifting the wig into the air. Margaret stared at her with wide eyes, the sort of look on her face that one got when they knew they had been caught out. Jason put his hand on the cuffs on his belt and waited.

"You were Douglas Creel's lawyer," Wilma said. "You were the one that pointed out that someone in a blonde wig had been near him before he was found dead. You were planning on framing Nancy for all of this. The only thing I can't figure out is why. Why go through all this effort? Why kill Douglas and Richard?"

Margaret chuckled, her demeanor changing instantly. "I didn't kill them. And I might as well tell you everything. He will rise again and take me from jail soon enough. That little witch lied about her stepfather. Her testimony put him in jail but it was all a ruse. She was just after his money. After five years of rotting, he'd had enough. He reached out to me with a plan."

"To destroy Nancy's life once and for all," Wilma murmured.

Margaret smiled and nodded. "Exactly. Using my connections, I was able to smuggle Richard to the jail and use an old trick of theirs, playing double, to help break Douglas out of jail. We knew we didn't have much time and so then put everything into play. Richard would pose as Douglas while Douglas prepared himself. Then, when everyone thought Nancy had murdered her stepfather, she would be sent away and my Douglas would be free."

Wilma shared an alarmed look with Jason.

Jason stepped forward. "How could you do that, when Douglas was dead?"

"You don't understand. We slit his throat and used a silver dagger to stab him. But that doesn't kill a vampire," Margaret said, shaking her head. "It was just to set the stage. And it was very convincing, wasn't it? He really did seem dead. But he wasn't. And I know he wasn't because he visited me last night."

Wilma shuddered, alarm coursing through her as Margaret caressed the small puncture marks in her neck. Did she really believe what she was saying, or was she making up a story to make herself look insane?

"But that doesn't explain why you would be part of it," Wilma said. Her voice shook slightly.

Margaret shook her head. "It's simple, really. As I was dealing with the little witch during the trial, I could see what Douglas told me was true. She really was a wicked thing. Cursed and lying. She deserved to be put away instead of him. And for my faithfulness, Douglas will give me a gift. He will restore my youth and allow me to live forever."

She stroked the punctures in her neck again, a blissful smile on her face. Wilma could hardly believe what she was hearing. After everything that happened in the case, she hadn't been expecting this! It seemed to be too bizarre to be true. And yet... she remembered the fangs in Douglas's mouth. The clean blade stuck between his ribs.

Even if he had been killed after escaping the prison, there still wasn't enough time for them to pull off everything in a single night. It was too complex, especially when it came to the bloodless body. What if...

No, she told herself firmly. *Douglas was out of jail for much longer than a single night. That's what Margaret said. Richard took his place. He pretended to be Douglas in jail. It must have been for a few days at least.*

Douglas had been dead for a lot longer than they realized. He had to have been. It still sent chills down Wilma's spine to hear just how convinced of herself that Margaret was. It seemed impossible that she would really believe such an outlandish story, and yet there was nothing but conviction in Margaret's eyes.

Jason cleared his throat. "So let me get this straight. You and Richard broke Douglas out of jail, and then you cut Douglas's throat and drained his blood so that you could then put the blood in Nancy's house to make it look like she killed him, all the while knowing that since Douglas is a vampire he'd just heal from the injuries?"

"Of course. We wanted to make sure Nancy knew that we were coming after her, too. Wanted her to know that her curse had caught up and that she was next."

"Why not just kill her?" Wilma asked.

Margaret shook her head. "Because then she would be a vampire, too. Don't you see? It's in the family."

"But Nancy isn't related to the Creels by blood," Jason said.

"That's what she wanted to believe."

Wilma swallowed hard. "Alright. Say we believe you. You then had Richard at the party in that mask and that getup to frighten Nancy, hoping to drive her away so you could then wear the wig and frame her for Douglas's death. But you judged wrong, and since she was right next to me when the body was found, you had to improvise. That's why you killed Richard, isn't it?"

"I didn't kill him," Margaret replied serenely. "Douglas bit him. I gave him the morphine to help ease the pain of the transformation. Just wait. You'll find their bodies leave the morgue soon enough. Then they will come to me and I will be young and immortal forever!"

She threw back her head, laughing. Wilma shared another glance with Jason as Jason took the handcuffs off his belt.

"Margaret Lowell, you are under—"

"Arrest," Margaret interrupted. She held out her thin wrists, smiling and laughing still. "But not for long, Detective. Not for long."

———

"I don't know how to thank you," Nancy said gratefully. She wrapped her arms around herself as she shivered. "I knew that

Douglas was obsessed with the occult and supernatural, but I had no idea that his delusions went so deep. How could he have convinced someone like Margaret about it? And to think, both brothers willingly died because they were so certain they were vampires…"

She shook her head, her eyebrows knit together. Wilma agreed with her. The whole thing had left a chill in her bones.

"It's over now," she assured the younger woman. "Margaret is in jail. Nobody will be coming after you again."

"Thank you. I feel like a weight has been lifted off me," Nancy sighed. "It feels like I'm finally free. Ever since my mother met Douglas, he's been this looming shadow. Now, I can finally feel the sunlight again."

Wilma smiled and gave the younger woman a hug. As she left the house, she pondered on this case. It had been one of the strangest she'd helped to solve. She still wasn't sure that Margaret believed what she was saying, or if there had been other motives behind her actions that they would never find out.

As she walked along the sidewalk, the trees bare of their leaves and the chill of autumn changing to the cold of winter, Wilma realized that it didn't matter. Margaret was in jail. It was like what Nancy had said, they were free of the case. Even if things didn't resolve quite the way Wilma wished they would, it was over.

She let out a breath, which misted in the air. It was time to take down the Halloween decorations and get back to normal life.

EPILOGUE

WILMA WADE BENT over her spiral-bound notebook, scribbling frantically as she tried to capture the words that had popped into her mind as she waited for Detective Jason Fellow at the local coffee spot. She had arrived fifteen minutes early, having misjudged how long it would take her to walk here from her home. Her mind had been filled all day with this new story, and she wanted to get all the details just right.

"Miss Wade. I hope I'm not interrupting," Jason said as he slid into the booth.

"One moment," she said, not looking up.

She finished off her page, chewed on her pencil for a moment, then wrote one more paragraph. Finished, she smiled to herself as she packed away her notebook. "Sorry for my rudeness. I just have to get that out of my system."

"It's perfectly alright," Jason said. He folded his hands over the table. "Sorry I'm late. I had some paperwork for the Douglas Creel case to take care of. Nancy has officially been cleared of all charges and Margaret is in custody, awaiting trial. The DA is certain this will be an open-and-shut case."

"Good." Wilma nodded her approval.

Jason ordered a coffee and tapped his fingers on the table, a slightly troubled expression on his face. "There's just one thing that is a little… strange. It's regarding Douglas Creel's body."

Wilma leaned forward, her interest piqued. "What do you mean?"

"Well… it's a funny thing. His body was claimed from the morgue last night. Only, the people who claimed him weren't family members according to the paperwork. It was all in order, but it's strange that they would come so late at night," Jason said slowly.

"Maybe they were just too busy?" Wilma suggested. It was strange but there was any number of reasons why the body would be collected at night. "Maybe they had a long drive. Do you know where they were taking him?"

Jason shook his head slowly. "They didn't leave any sort of forwarding address. I took a look at the business card they left, but there was no contact information. The morgue attendants described them as being very pale, very serious, and all dressed in strange clothes. Old-fashioned suits and the like. One even wore sunglasses, even though it was night."

Wilma shivered. "That is strange."

"Yeah. The attendants all said they were unnerved about the situation and they even caught one of them staring at a fresh body with what they described as a hungry look." Jason rubbed his chin, frowning. "They could be mistaken, of course. It was a strange case and with everything else that has been going on, it's understandable to get the jitters."

"Of course."

"The person wearing sunglasses was probably high or had sensitivity to lights. The fluorescents can hurt," he added.

Wilma prided herself on being a reasonable person. She wasn't given to flights of fancy and even with her writer's imagination, she always had both feet planted firmly on the ground. Which was why she was surprised when a chill ran down her spine. She gazed out to the fall evening, searching the lengthening shadows among the orange leaves.

"What about Richard Creel's body?" Wilma asked.

Jason shook his head slowly. "They didn't want him. Only Douglas."

"Maybe..." she said slowly, lowering her voice as she did so, "Maybe Douglas Creel really was a vampire."

She looked back at Jason. Both of them stared at each other, serious and locked in the possibilities. Could it be? The whole case was so strange. They never had figured out how Margaret managed to get a bloodless body into the middle of a crowded party with nobody noticing it...

Jason chuckled suddenly. The moment was broken. Wilma shook her head and rolled her eyes at herself and they both leaned back, enjoying the cheerful glow of the café.

"Maybe he was a vampire. Maybe he actually turned into a bat and flew away," Jason said.

"Maybe if we look up the town records, we'll find a five-hundred-year-old portrait of a man that looks exactly like him," Wilma joked.

Jason chuckled. "What are you writing anyway?"

Wilma pulled her notebook to her chest. "Oh, just a little mystery about a strange man, a gothic castle, and a woman my age who nobody believes when she starts seeing strange things around town."

"Sounds intriguing. I'd love to read it when it's done."

"You'll be the first one," Wilma promised. "But I have to write it first!"

The End

MURDER AT THE MANOR

A SMALL-TOWN NEW YEAR'S COZY MYSTERY WITH A SENIOR SLEUTH

CHAPTER ONE

WILMA WADE always enjoyed the weeks leading up to Christmas. The beginning of December represented a shift in the air, a change as the year came to a close. It was a great time to reflect on the past and start to think about what goals would be good for the coming year. The only thing she didn't like was how the cold made her bones ache.

"Welcome to Winter's Edge, Miss Wade." Jacob Howell, a local historian, took her coat in the foyer of the old house.

"Thank you," Wilma said.

She rubbed her hands together, grateful for the warmth. The old house, Winter's Edge, had always been beautiful but it had fallen into a state of disrepair. Jacob had spent the last few years doing major fundraisers to restore the old place. It had paid off for sure.

"I wanted to thank you again for all the help you have been, researching my book," Wilma said to Jacob. "I sent it off to ten publishers last month. So far nothing back but I'm hopeful."

Jacob beamed. "I was happy to help."

"So, this is the house that you told me about, right?" Wilma asked as she took off her coat. "The one I based my murder mystery on?"

"It is. This was one of the first large houses to be built in Barwick," Jacob told her, stowing her coat in the closet. "There were rumors that it held a major speakeasy during Prohibition, not to mention lots of shady dealings that the family was meant to be involved in. I've been writing a book about it while overseeing the renovations."

"A speakeasy?" Wilma's interest was piqued. "Did you find any evidence of that during the renovation?"

Jacob's eyes sparkled as he led her toward the parlor. "We didn't find the room itself, but we did find several old tunnels. They didn't lead anywhere, but we haven't finished all of the renovations yet. That's one of the reasons I'm doing this open house for the police department. I'm hoping to raise enough funds for the next stage."

Wilma shook her head, amazed. "You are very dedicated to your work, Mr. Howell. I admire your ability to stick with it."

Jacob smiled at her as they entered the parlor, where there were already several other people waiting. "I loved this place as a kid. I used to sneak in with my friends. We'd put on our own speakeasies, so to say. I remember the times when we would put on our boom boxes and listen to the music as we danced and drank."

"Well, I don't condone underage drinking or trespassing," Wilma said, a teasing glint in her eye. "But I can see how this would hold a lot of good memories. I'm surprised, though. Aren't there any family members left?"

"The house was abandoned years ago. The town took over ownership," Jacob answered brightly.

He left her then, going to talk with other people. Wilma took in the sight of the parlor. The house had been only minimally decorated. Most of the furniture and fixings were kept off-site for restoration. There were a few couches sitting in the parlor and a large refreshment table. There were even waiters wandering around serving glasses of red wine.

Wilma snagged herself a glass and sipped it. It tasted delicious and she sighed happily.

There were a bunch people from the police department already here. It was a special tour for the department, with Wilma being an honorary guest. Wilma was just disappointed that Detective Jason Fellow had to work and couldn't be part of the festivities tonight. She was hesitant about participating in an event for the department without him.

"Miss Wade," a cool voice said to her side.

Wilma recognized it. She bit back a groan of dismay when she turned to Detective Anne Harper, a middle-aged woman with light brown hair and judgmental eyes. Her expression made it excessively clear that she didn't think that Wilma had any business being here tonight.

Wilma had always thought that the adage, 'Kill them with kindness' was a good way to go through life. She wasn't the sort to engage in petty squabbles, and certainly didn't go out of her way to be catty to other people. Anne Harper always tested her patience in ways that were most unladylike. She let out a short huff before she could stop herself, then plastered on a polite smile.

"Hello, Detective. I was under the impression you would be working tonight," Wilma said, keeping her tone as pleasant as possible, given the circumstances. "It looks like it's going to be quite the fun party, don't you think?"

Anne's lips thinned as she looked Wilma over. "I was under the impression that this was for members of the police department and their families. Have you adopted Jason Fellow, then?"

Wilma forced herself not to react to the blatant rudeness. "Your Captain gave me his personal invitation to join tonight's tour. If you have a problem with me being here, you should take it up with him."

She turned and walked away, unwilling to continue to defend

herself against the woman who didn't want her there. Anne had brought up concerns to the department several times about Wilma. She didn't think that a civilian should be so involved in cases, and that the department gave her and Jason too much leeway.

Over the Easter holiday, there had been an assassination attempt on Wilma. She had been given a poisoned chocolate egg. Wilma luckily figured out that it was a trap before she ate the egg. But Anne had used the incident to double-down on trying to get Wilma barred from helping Detective Fellow in his investigations.

Wilma pushed those thoughts aside and focused on the others in the room. She spotted Norman Prose, one of the detectives nearing retirement age. He caught her eye and smiled pleasantly. Wilma joined him and his wife.

"Detective Prose, Mrs. Prose," she greeted. "Lovely house, isn't it?"

"I suppose," Norman said, sipping his glass of wine.

Mrs. Prose, whose name Wilma shamefully couldn't remember at the moment, giggled. "Norman wouldn't have come if it had been up to him. I had to drag him here."

"Tours of old houses aren't my forte," Norman said, looking bold.

"It doesn't help that Jacob Howell is running the tour. He was our neighbor a few years back," Mrs. Prose explained, wrinkling her nose. "And not a very good one."

Norman laughed. "Jenny, I'm certain Miss Wade doesn't need to hear about all of that."

"Norman, I'm just saying," Jenny Prose said with a roll of her eyes.

"What are we talking about?" David Reardon, a handsome detective on the verge of retirement, sidled up to the group. He had an empty wine glass in one hand and a full one in the other. He grinned at them all, and his smile widened further with he saw Wilma. "Ah, Wilma, I'm so glad that you were able to come to our little tour group. My, my, but you look wonderful tonight."

He gave her a charming wink. David had been widowed for something like ten years now. Wilma smiled and laughed at his polite flirting. He had always struck her as a rather happy man, eager to elicit a laugh from others. He was the sort of man that put others at ease.

"Jenny and I have to go speak with the commissioner," Norman said. He nodded at the both of them as he headed away.

Wilma turned to David. "What's this I hear about you retiring in the New Year?"

"Well, I'm retiring in the New Year," David answered teasingly. "I've been giving it a lot of thought and it's time to hang it up. I'm going to take up gardening and finally have some time to go fishing. Though I can't tell you that it's been easy."

"I remember when I retired. It was a very emotional decision," Wilma said.

David nodded, looking serious for a minute but then his usual smile came back. "Say, why don't you and I escape this little party and go look for that speakeasy? I hear that the owners had just gotten in a shipment of the finest brandy just before they were closed down, and there are crates and crates of it still in there."

"Oh?" Wilma laughed. "Well, I do like a mystery."

"I know. And, uh…" He blushed as he shifted from foot to foot. "I was thinking, once I'm officially retired, maybe you and I could go for a coffee some time. I've got a bunch of old cases I thought maybe you could help me whip into some sort of written format."

Wilma's eyes widened. "You mean like a date?"

"Well… yeah," David said, giving her a surprisingly shy grin.

"Oh." Wilma's cheeks warmed. She had been on a date or two in the last few decades, but since the death of her fiancé, she hadn't felt the desire for any sort of romantic relationship. Was it time for her to start thinking about dating in earnest?

"Dad, there you are," a young woman said. She came over to David and looped her arm around his. "The tour is about to start."

"Ah, good." He smiled at Wilma as his daughter pulled him away. "I'll see you later, Miss Wade."

Wilma nodded. As Jacob called for everyone to gather around, she reached into her purse for a mint. The wine was delicious, but had left her throat a little dry. Her fingers closed around something large and round. She didn't have anything like that in her purse. Frowning, Wilma pulled the item out.

It was a chocolate egg.

CHAPTER TWO

WILMA STARED at the chocolate egg in her hand, her eyes wide and her heart pounding. It wasn't just any chocolate egg, something to be forgotten for months before randomly being found.

No. This was the egg.

The poisoned egg that had been given to her at Easter. The one that had been meant to kill her. Her breathing became rapid as she shoved it back into her purse and zipped it shut. She looked up, gazing around at the police in the room. She hadn't been paying attention to her purse, half-open, on her shoulder. She'd been so distracted by talking to people that anyone could have put that egg into her purse.

The egg that had been collected as evidence at Easter, only to disappear from the evidence lockup in July. She and Jason had deduced at that time that whoever took it had to be part of the police department, but they hadn't been able to pinpoint anyone as a suspect. Now it just happened to show up in her purse, at an event full of police?

No. This was deliberate. This was a warning.

The problem was, what was it a warning for? She followed

along on the edge of the police group as Jacob started the tour, talking about the family that had originally owned the house. They had apparently been quite the crime family back in the day. Wilma could hardly pay attention. It had been a month since she last was involved in a case. Was whoever gave her the egg ramping up to something?

Maybe it was something else. Maybe the killer was just reminding her that they were watching. After all, if they wanted to kill her still, wouldn't they have poisoned her wine glass, rather than leave the egg in her purse?

It was all very unnerving, regardless. Wilma glanced around at the gathered cops, making sure she didn't seem too conspicuous. Most everyone was paying attention to Jacob, while others were looking at the architecture or reading pamphlets. David Reardon caught her eye and smiled. Wilma smiled back, though her heart wasn't in it.

Could he have put the egg in her purse? Was his flirting just to catch her off guard? It hurt more than she cared to admit, that it could have been just a show and that he wasn't sincere in his interest for her. But he wasn't the only one with opportunity. Anybody in the house could have slipped her the egg, even Jacob.

Wilma squared her shoulders. She would remain on her guard, but she wasn't going to end up terrified about this. No, she wasn't going to be frightened off. There was a new mystery here and she was going to face it head-on.

Jacob led them up a wide set of stairs that curved to one side. It was the sort of staircase that Wilma used to dream about sliding down as a little girl. Now, she was too worried about the seemingly innocuous chocolate egg to even enjoy it.

"This is the library," Jacob said, gesturing to a closed door. "While I would love to continue the tour, the library unfortunately hasn't been fully restored yet. This is one of the reasons why I appreciate you all coming here tonight. I am holding a fundraiser later this week to start raising money to restore the library... and reveal all the secrets therein."

There was polite laughter in response. Jacob told them all that there were refreshments in the Great Hall, and that he would be back down in half an hour.

"I just have some business to take care of," he said.

As she made her way back down the stairs, Wilma made small talk with the various detectives and their family members. None of them acted suspicious. Eventually, she slipped into the bathroom, locked the door, and called Jason.

"Miss Wade," he greeted. "I wasn't expecting to hear from you."

"We have a problem," she told him grimly.

Wilma told Jason what happened as concisely as possible. When she was done, he let out a heavy sigh.

"Are you okay?" he asked worriedly.

"I am. I haven't eaten or drunk anything since I found the egg. I'm certain it's meant to frighten me. I just can't figure out what they're trying to frighten me away from," she answered. Her mind flickered to Anne Harper, the detective who didn't want her to be anywhere near the precinct or the cases that Wilma solved with Jason. Could it be her? Was she trying to get Wilma to leave the department?

"I'm on my way over," Jason said, his voice grim. "Make sure you keep hold of that purse. I'm going to bring a fingerprint kit with me so we can dust it. With any luck, we'll be able to pick up a print off it. Do you have an evidence baggie that you can put it in until I get there?"

Wilma sat on the closed toilet and carefully opened up one of the side pockets. "I always carry a couple with me these days."

"Good. Bag up the egg. I'll get there as soon as I can."

They hung up and Wilma carefully bagged the egg. She hoped that walking around with the tour hadn't smudge any fingerprints that might be on it. But, given that this was a cop they were dealing with, she very much doubted they would find any prints. All the same—

A scream echoed in the mansion. Wilma jumped. She sealed the evidence bag and dropped it back into her purse, quickly zipping it shut again before she left the bathroom. Everyone was moving toward the stairs. Wilma slipped her way through the crowd, up the stairs, and down the hall. She approached the room where the screams had fallen silent. It was the library, with dark shelves full of books behind glass doors.

Jacob Howell lay face-down on the floor, a glass of wine clutched in her hand, its contents spilling over the rug. Wilma's breath caught in her chest as she noted the blue lips and foam tinging them. Poison. She thought of the egg in her purse and suddenly felt dizzy.

Kneeling next to the body was Rosie Reardon, tears streaming down her face as she clutched at Jacob's jacket. David pushed through and wrapped his arms around his daughter.

"He's gone, Rosie. Let him go. Let me get you out of here," he murmured, soft and gentle.

"I called the precinct," Anne Harper said nearby. "They're sending Detective Fellow and a forensic team. Let's back away, keep the scene clear." Her gaze landed on Wilma and her eyes narrowed.

"I'm going to go with Miss Reardon and see if I can help her at all," Wilma said, feeling the need to tell Detective Harper her movements, as though she was a suspect.

Anne nodded curtly at her.

As she was turning to go, Wilma spied a notebook tucked behind a bookcase near the entrance to the library. None of the police had seen it, so Wilma took out a second evidence bag, scooped up the notebook, and slipped it into her purse. Nobody paid attention to her, and it was a good thing, too. Wilma's gut told her that the notebook had something to do with the murder, and it would be difficult to explain why she had to hold onto it rather than giving it to one of the cops.

Any one of these people could be a killer. Until Jason arrived, she couldn't trust anyone. For all she knew, if she handed over evidence it would mysteriously go missing.

Next, Wilma slipped out of the room. She could still hear Rosie's sobs and followed the noise down to the parlor on the main floor. There, David helped her to sit in a chair and retrieved a glass of wine, only to hesitate and sniff it.

Wilma cleared her throat. "I think it's probably best if we all avoid eating or drinking anything. We don't know if anything else has been poisoned," she said.

David jumped, turning toward her. His expression was somber, most unlike the usual jovial expression he wore. He nodded once to her. "You're right about that. We can't assume that Jacob was the only intended victim, at least not yet."

At this, Rosie let out a whimper. She rocked back and forth, her hands pressed to her lips and tears falling down her face. "He said that he'd found how to get into the speakeasy," she whispered. "He was going to show it to me."

Wilma sat next to Rosie and took her hand. "Were you and Jacob involved?"

"Oh." Rosie's cheek reddened and she ducked her head. "Well, not officially. We'd been seeing each other a little over the last few months. It wasn't anything serious, though. We were just... spending time with each other."

Wilma glanced at David; did he know about his daughter's involvement with the victim? He patted her shoulder, his expression giving nothing away.

A throat cleared at the door. Anne Harper stood in the doorway, looking in at them. She gazed over Rosie and David with a calculating look before her gaze flickered to Wilma. Her lips thinned. Her eyes were sharp like knives directed at Wilma.

"Miss Wade, can I speak with you?" Detective Harper asked. Her voice was thick and brusque.

"Of course." Wilma stepped out into the hallway.

Anne folded her arms as she lowered her voice. "Because I know I need to say it, stay out of this investigation. You were here along with the rest of us and are therefore a suspect. If I learn that you've done anything to interfere, you can believe me when I say I will make certain the captain forbids Detective Fellow from working with you again."

Wilma thought about the notebook in her purse and kept her expression smooth. "You are a suspect, too. How do I know you're not trying to warn me off, so that I don't help catch you?"

"I didn't kill him," Anne hissed.

"And I," Wilma said, "will not interfere with Detective Fellow's case. I will, however, help him as long as he sees fit."

Anne lowered her voice. "You'd better watch yourself, Miss Wade. I'm not the only one that wants to see you gone."

She walked away, leaving Wilma unsettled. Gone as in, no longer investigating? Or gone as in... dead?

CHAPTER THREE

DETECTIVE JASON FELLOW arrived at Winter's Edge quickly. Wilma wondered who all would understand that he got here too quickly for him to have left after he heard about the murder. Judging by the suspicious glance Anne Harper gave her, Wilma suspected that she might. But she ignored the look as she went to greet Jason.

"Wilma. Are you alright?" Jason asked, looking at her worriedly.

"I'm fine, Detective. I was in the bathroom when I heard the screams." There had been some time between the end of the tour and when the body was found, though, and Wilma wasn't sure when the time of death had been pinpointed to, so she added, "After the tour was done, I was here in the Great Hall until I went into the bathroom. I can give you their names. I know it's important to make sure everyone's alibis line up."

Jason nodded. "Thank you. The others will be here soon. In the meantime, I'd like to take a look at the crime scene."

Anne stepped up beside him. "This way, Detective."

She led him to the library with Wilma tailing behind. Once in the library, Jason took pictures of the scene, then picked up the glass Jason was drinking from. He sniffed it experimentally and grimaced.

"That smells awful," he said as he bagged it. "It makes me wonder how Jacob couldn't have known he was drinking poison."

Anne, who had been standing in the doorway, folded her arms. "Detective Fellow, I think it only right to tell you that after the tour was over, I came to speak with the victim. He poured me a glass of wine from the same bottle and we spoke for about five minutes before I returned to the Great Hall."

"Why were you in the library?" Jason asked, all business.

"I left my phone in here while we were on the tour. When I came in, Jacob said he was just taking a breather and would be back down soon," Anne answered. "He was drinking from his glass but showed no signs of poisoning. He started to talk about the speakeasy that was supposedly here and I made my excuses to leave."

Wilma found this interesting. Most people she knew had a fascination with speakeasies and the undercurrent of rebellion during Prohibition. "Oh? You don't like speakeasies, then?"

Anne gave her a hard look. "Speakeasies were flouting the law. I'm the sort of cop that believes in upholding the law. I don't think we should glamorize criminals. What people forget is that it wasn't all flapper dresses and charming nightclubs. There was murder involved. Murder, drugs, violence. That's not something I want to celebrate."

"I can see your point," Wilma agreed. "I don't think there is any harm in learning more about the past, though. Jacob seemed to be very enthusiastic about the speakeasy, but he certainly didn't shy away from the other criminal endeavors of the family. When I asked for his help researching my book, he told me all sorts of things they used to do."

"Perhaps not. But that doesn't mean I wanted to listen to him rattle on about it," Anne said. "Anyway, I passed David Reardon on the way back down to the Great Hall."

"Thank you, Detective," Jason said as he made a note in his notebook. "Did you drink the wine that Jacob gave you?"

"I did. But I put the glass down in the parlor and I wouldn't be able to point it out." Anne frowned as she folded her arms. "Would it be alright if I had someone drive me to the hospital to check me out? We don't know what sort of poison it was."

Jason nodded. "Go ahead. I'll have our techs analyze this glass at once. I don't want to cause a panic, but it's best to know if anyone else might have been poisoned."

Anne gave a sharp nod and headed out. Wilma watched her go, wondering if this was a killer making her escape. She followed Jason as they found David Reardon. Despite having been tipsy earlier in the party, he was noticeably sober now. He was still in the parlor with Rosie.

"Detective Reardon, Miss Reardon," Jason greeted, bowing his head to them. "I need to ask you both some questions. Detective, may I speak with you privately?"

David's hand tightened on Rosie's shoulder. "Whatever you need to ask Rosie, you can say it in front of me."

Wilma shook her head. "He wasn't asking to talk with Rosie privately, David. He was asking to speak with you."

Both David and Rosie looked startled. Then David shot Rosie a worried look while Rosie just looked confused. "Why do you need to talk to my father? He wasn't there."

"We have a witness who saw him go into the library shortly before you found the body," Wilma told her. She sat by the younger woman and put a careful arm around her shoulder.

David shifted from foot to foot, looking anywhere but Rosie.

"Detective," Jason said sternly. "What business did you have with the victim?"

Finally, David looked back at him. He hesitated, seeming to weigh his options, before he sighed. "Rosie, I know that you and

Jacob were more than casually seeing each other. I know that he proposed to you."

Rosie's cheeks went red. "How—?"

"I'm a Detective." David gave her a small smile. "I know why you didn't tell me. I haven't gotten along with Mr. Howell," he told Jason, shaking his head. "I thought he wasn't good enough for my daughter. But I was willing to bury the hatchet. I might not like him that much, but he treated Rosie with respect and made her happy. I went to tell him I knew, and that while I might not be happy about it, they could have my blessing. I wanted him to know. I planned on talking to Rosie tonight after we got home."

Rosie's eyes filled with fresh tears. "Oh, Dad. I didn't like hiding it from you."

David patted her hand. "I know."

"How long would you say you spoke with him?" Jason asked.

"Ten or fifteen minutes. I thought I saw someone outside the door when I left but I didn't see who it was."

"Thank you," Jason said.

He and Jason went to speak with the other guests. Soon, they had everyone accounted for except Norman Prose, who Officer Hendrick saw slip into the kitchen and not return until after the body was found.

"I was feeling a bit peckish, so I raided the fridge. Check the video cameras, you'll see I was in the kitchen until after the body was found," Norman said, calm but disinterested.

Wilma studied him. There was a certain casualness about his words that she was uncertain of. But then, if he was telling the truth, there would be no need for him to be anything but casual. And he didn't have much of a motive—being upset that a few years ago he had a bad neighbor wasn't exactly reason to kill someone!

"Detective, are we going to be kept here all night?" Norman complained. "I didn't even want to be here in the first place."

"All in good time, Detective," Jason answered. "I'm going to have to ask for your patience for a little while longer."

Norman sighed but nodded.

It didn't take long for the video feed to be found. Jason and Wilma reviewed it and found it was true. Norman had spent the entire time after the tour in the kitchen. Nobody else had gone in or out of the library. Which meant they only had three suspects. David, Rosie, and Anne.

Jason got a call from the lab. He listened to what they said, thanked them, and hung up. "We have the results on the tox screen."

Wilma's eyes widened. "That was fast."

"We needed fast results, just in case it was something everyone had been dosed with," Jason answered.

Wilma noted his turn of phrase and relaxed. "I'm guessing it wasn't something slipped into all of our wine."

Jason shook his head. "It's a very fast-acting poison, one that takes effect within seconds of being consumed. If anyone else had drunk something, they would be dead already. I'm sending a message to Anne to let her know there's nothing to worry about."

"And what about the smell? If that was the poison, wouldn't Jason have smelled it and not drank?" Wilma inquired.

"That's part of the poison's nature," Jason said grimly. "When it oxidizes, it smells strongly. Which means Jacob would have had to consume the poisoned wine quickly after it was administered."

"Which means it couldn't have been planted earlier," Wilma murmured. She frowned. "David went into the library after Anne. Doesn't that mean that she couldn't have killed him?"

Jason looked grim. "Perhaps. Or it could mean they were in on it together."

Wilma shivered. One killer cop was bad enough, but two? She took a deep breath, steadying herself. "I found something in the library I thought you should see," she said, and pulled the notebook out of her purse.

CHAPTER FOUR

JASON CAREFULLY DUSTED THE NOTEBOOK, finding only one set of fingerprints. He sent them to be analyzed, but they were likely to be Jacob's prints.

"Let's see what this is, shall we?" Jason asked.

He opened the book and Wilma leaned in, her eyes skimming the pages. It was filled with meticulous notes on the history of Winter's Edge, including several ornate drawings. Wilma was impressed with how much detail was in the sketches. She recognized a few of them as moldings in the library, as well as the massive hearth.

"What's that there?" Wilma peered closer at a page. "It seems as though when the police were cracking down on the original family, their youngest son disappeared. Only a bloody handkerchief was found in his bedroom."

Jason read the page. "It doesn't have much to do with our current murder."

"Yes, but it's great fodder for a story," Wilma said eagerly. She skimmed the page quickly. "Jacob theorized that the son... Is that Stephen?"

Jason squinted. "Looks like it. Stephen Henderson."

"Faked his death and made off with the books that the family used for their criminal empire and kept building his wealth in secret." Wilma leaned back on her heels, imagining the story possibilities. Her fingers itched for a pen.

"Regardless, it doesn't help with our investigation," Jason said. He bagged the notebook again. "I'll have people look through it, but it seems to only be about the history of Winter's Edge." He glanced at the door and turned more fully to Wilma. "Let me see the chocolate egg."

Wilma blinked. She'd nearly forgotten about the egg. Quickly, she dug it out of her purse and handed it to Jason. He pulled it out of the bag and dusted it, but other than a couple of badly smudged prints, where Wilma was sure she had grabbed it, there was nothing. It had been a long shot anyway. Jason placed the egg with the rest of the evidence.

"It will be harder for the killer to sneak it out now," Jason said. He held the egg to his nose and sniffed it. "Wilma, do you smell that?"

She leaned forward and wrinkled her nose. "It's the same scent as the poison in the wine. It must have taken longer for the egg to oxidize because it's wrapped in the foil."

Jason's eyes were bright. "It also means that whoever meant to kill you would have had to poison the egg quickly before it got to you. I'll be able to go back over the old parade tapes and see if any of our current suspects were there that day."

"We have some evidence the two crimes are connected," Wilma agreed with a nod. "But I don't see how. I didn't know Jacob at all. Why would the same person want to kill us both?"

"Let's go back to the library. Maybe there are more clues there," Jason suggested as he rubbed his chin.

As they headed for the library, though, Anne Harper found them. She looked annoyed and tired. Her hair had been curled and styled earlier, but now it was pulled back into a tight bun, giving her a harsh, severe look. She had changed her clothes, too, dressed now in a sleek power suit. Wilma had to admit, Anne looked very intimidating like this.

"I thought you went to the hospital," Wilma said, surprised to see her.

Anne quirked one eyebrow at her. "After Detective Fellow let me know that I was safe, I decided to come back and lend whatever help I can. You've certainly cleared me by this time, as David Reardon entered the library after me. Which means I left Jacob alive."

"Unless you and David are in cahoots," Wilma said. "Or perhaps you gave him the poison and he drank it after David left."

She wasn't sure how quickly it oxidized, but there was a detail that Anne shouldn't know about.

Anne frowned but nodded. "Those are excellent points, Miss Wade. I know I'm innocent but you have to think of all possibilities."

Wilma's lips quirked, uncertain how to take Anne's change. That sounded almost like a compliment. Was she trying to butter her up?

"You should know that Norman and his wife are trying to bully the uniformed officers into letting them leave," Anne added. "I tried to talk to him, but you know Norman."

Jason sighed. "I do. Stay out here while I go deal with it." He caught Wilma's eye. "You're free to search the library for hidden passages."

He headed off and Anne stared at Wilma, her jaw open. "Hidden passages?"

Wilma shook her head, smiling to herself. "Detective Fellow knows me too well. Jacob was telling me that this old place is riddled with secret passages. One of them has to lead to the speakeasy. And if there is a passage that leads to the library, it opens up our suspect pool. Jacob's notebook had some drawings about the hearth. I think he suspected that there was a passageway connected to it."

Anne frowned. "That's quite a leap, Miss Wade."

"Is it really? There were passages found already, but the speakeasy hasn't been discovered. The library hasn't had any major renovations done. Jacob was looking for more funds to continue the restoration project," Wilma explained.

"I see." Anne's frown deepened as she shook her head. "Look. I think you're a terrific writer and I appreciate that you've helped Jason solve several cases. I just don't think it's a good idea for you to keep involving yourself. Someone already tried to kill you with that stunt in Easter. Do you know what sort of nightmare it will be for the department if they succeed next time?"

Next time. Wilma thought of the egg that had been dropped into her purse. Could Anne have put it there? She seemed like an obvious suspect, with her hostility toward Wilma... perhaps too obvious, really. If she was trying to kill Wilma, wouldn't she want to be friendly, to hide her motives?

Wilma kept an eye on Anne as she went into the library. Anne stood in the doorway, still frowning, watching her. It was unnerving to say the least. Wilma tried to put it out of her mind as she searched along the fireplace molding, though she wasn't sure what she was looking for. Finally, she saw a small reddish stain in the otherwise white molding. It looked like rust.

Of course! If there was a secret mechanism that opened a passageway, it would have rusted over time. Wilma held her breath and depressed the space in the middle of the stain. It groaned, but pressed inward.

There was a click and a bookcase to the left of the fireplace swung out. Wilma hurried to it, pushing it open wider.

"You found it," Anne cried out in disbelief. She hurried over and inspected the secret doorway. "Look at these hinges. They've been recently oiled. So, someone did know about this entrance."

"It might be Jacob," Wilma said.

Anne nodded, then whispered, "Or it might be the killer."

The two women stared at each other for a moment before Anne pulled a flashlight from her belt and flicked it on. Wilma thought about going back to get Jason, but Anne was already heading into the passageway and she didn't want to be left behind.

It was old, yes, and there were places in the walls, floor, and ceiling that were showing signs of disrepair, but it was also far cleaner than Wilma had expected.

"It looks like someone came through with a broom and cleaned up the cobwebs," Wilma said.

"More than that. Do you smell lemons?" Anne asked, sniffing.

Wilma did likewise. Yes, there was a faint trace of lemons in the air. "So, unless the killer went through in here with a cleaner, I think we can safely assume Jacob found the passage. He must have spent a few days cleaning it up so he could have a romantic date with Rosie in the speakeasy."

After some time, they found their way down a flight of stairs into a large, empty space. The theory about Jacob setting it up for a date was all but confirmed. The speakeasy had new electric lights installed, and there was a single table set up with a plaid tablecloth and a bottle of wine on it.

Anne went for the shelves of bottles lining the wall. She whistled. "Take a look at these bottles. Brandy. Whiskey. They've got to be worth hundreds now."

Wilma stepped up to the table. There was a small folder on it, filled with photocopies of old newspaper clippings. One of them held a picture of the original owners of Winter's Edge. The photo was blurry, but as she studied it, one of the faces leapt out to her. It looked vaguely familiar…

The door to the passageway swung shut.

CHAPTER FIVE

"IT WON'T BUDGE," Anne declared. She wiped the sweat from her brow as she glared at the sealed door. "How long do you think it will take Detective Fellow to find us?'

Wilma had been checking her phone unsuccessfully to see if she had gotten a signal. She tucked it away and turned back to Anne. "He'll find us. I'm sure he will."

Anne started to walk slowly around the room. "If there's one thing old Hollywood taught me, it's that these things always had two entrances. Let's look for a second one."

Wilma nodded. It made sense that the second entrance would be hidden. That way, if the police raided and found the speakeasy, the partiers would be able to hide away somewhere else. As she searched the walls, Wilma kept thinking about the photo of the original owners. She was certain that one person looked familiar, but who? It was so long ago, she wouldn't have been able to meet him herself... could she?

She noticed a slight scrape on the floor, a place where some sawdust had fallen near the wall. She bent to it and touched the dust. It was fresh, as though it was made by moving a door that didn't fully fit its frame from years of disuse. Peering at the panel above it, she found a slight crack, one that didn't fit with the rest of the wall.

"Here it is!" she cried out in delight. Anne joined her and together, they managed to pry open the second entrance.

The passage beyond this one was dusty, filled with cobwebs and mouse droppings. Wilma shuddered.

"There are footprints in the dust," Anne pointed out. "Walk carefully on the side, so we don't disturb them." They started down the hallway. Wilma stayed close to Anne with the flashlight. After a moment, Anne cleared her throat. "You know, you're pretty good at this. I understand why Detective Fellow likes to work with you."

"Thank you," Wilma said.

They emerged in the kitchen. Voices came from the Great Hall. There, Jason was arranging search parties. When he saw Anne and Wilma, relief washed over his face. Wilma quickly told him what they found while her eyes scanned the crowd.

"I don't believe that the door just shut on its own," Wilma whispered. "I think someone closed it. Where's David Reardon?"

Jason frowned as he turned. He ordered for the team to document the dusty footprints as Wilma led him back to the library—so as not to disturb evidence in the kitchen passage—and they went back down to the speakeasy.

There, they found David Reardon. He had a duffle bag and was filling it with the bottles of alcohol lining the shelves.

"Stop right there, Detective," Jason said sternly.

David straightened, his eyes going wide. "This isn't what it looks like."

Anne folded her arms. "What it looks like is that you learned about the speakeasy and realized you could make a lot of money on this old liquor. But Jacob wouldn't let you take it so you killed him."

"No!" David shook his head firmly. "No, that's not it at all. I wouldn't have hurt him. I knew that Jacob found the speakeasy. But I didn't suggest he sell off the liquor. No, he was far too noble for that. History was his life and he wouldn't have sold it. I convinced him to have the tour so I would have a way to sneak in and steal it. I'm retiring but my finances... I don't have much to leave Rosie. I was hoping to get enough from the liquor that I could give her the down payment for a house. For her and Jacob," he added. "I didn't kill him. Rosie loves him. I would never hurt her like that."

"Take him away," Jason said to the uniformed officers.

They handcuffed David and led him back up the stairs toward the library. Anne frowned as she watched them go.

"I don't know if I buy his story," she said.

Jason ran a hand through his hair. "I'm inclined to believe him. What he says makes sense."

"You sure? Or is it just because we know him as our friend that you want to believe he's innocent?" Anne asked.

They shared a look. Wilma turned away to give them privacy. It was times like this that she understood why Anne didn't want her around. It was a betrayal that Wilma, not a cop herself, couldn't fully understand. But she had to agree with Detective Fellow. Wanting to steal the liquor wasn't a good enough reason to commit murder. If it had been, then wouldn't David have come down to steal the liquor right away?

She picked up the folder of Jason's notes again. "We know now that the library is connected to the kitchen. Norman Prose has to be put back on our list of suspects," she said.

"That's true," Anne said with a nod. She approached Wilma. "Is there anything of interest in there?"

"Maybe. It's this old photo. I swear I've seen this person before, but I can't remember when," Wilma said. She pointed at the man she was talking about. The more she stared at him, the more she was certain she was right—but still, she didn't have any clue as to who it might be.

Anne took it and frowned. "You're right, he does look familiar. Fellow, can you place him?"

Jason squinted at the photo. "Nope. I don't think he looks familiar at all."

"It's something in the shape of his jaw," Anne said slowly. "It's a nice jaw."

Jason turned to Wilma. "Norman doesn't have a motive to kill Jacob. They knew each other from a few years back, but that's not enough. And even if he knew about this place, it doesn't mean he's a killer. He might have had the same idea that David had about the liquor."

"Then our major suspects have to be Rosie or David," Wilma said. "But I just don't think either of them could be a killer."

Anne cleared her throat. "Can I take that as the 'Anne and David are in cahoots' theory is out of the window?"

"Technically, no," Jason admitted.

"For what it's worth, I don't think you're the killer," Wilma offered.

"That makes me feel so much better," Anne said sarcastically, but there was a clear loosening of her tense shoulders.

Wilma focused on the photo again. And suddenly, she knew exactly who it reminded her of. But as Anne pointed out, she was still a suspect. That meant she had to talk with Jason alone. How could she do that without tipping Anne off that she had made a breakthrough?

She cleared her throat and tucked the folder under her arm. "Do you mind if I take this home to keep studying, Detective Fellow? It has been an exhausting night and I feel like a cup of tea and my slippers are in order."

Jason nodded. "You're right. I think we've found all we can for now. Everyone will be allowed to return home."

"Thank you," Wilma said. She suddenly felt her age, all tired and worn-out. It had been an eventful night.

"You have your car?" Jason asked. "Or do I need to drive you home?"

Wilma hesitated. That would be the best way to speak with him alone, wouldn't it? But she did have her car… "Well, I drove myself here. But it might be good if you'd drive me, Detective. I'm awfully tired and I'm not sure it's safe for me to drive."

Anne gave her a suspicious look but didn't comment. Jason helped her with her coat and they headed out.

"I know who the photo reminds me of," she said once in Jason's cruiser.

His eyebrows knit together. "Who?"

"There's a photo of Norman's grandfather on his desk at the precinct. I'm sure it's the same man that's in this photo." Wilma's mind raced along the possibilities. "If Jacob discovered that Norman's grandfather was the missing heir, the one that escaped the police when the speakeasy was shut down, that means Norman might have something to lose if his family's dark past came to light."

Jason hummed as he drove along. "That doesn't make much sense, either. Norman can't be prosecuted for what his family did."

"But if he still has wealth from those family crimes, it might be taken from him to make restitution for the people his family hurt," Wilma pointed out. "Maybe Jacob contacted him, told him that he'd found a connection. And then Norman decided to get rid of him."

"I'll look into the crimes that the family committed," Jason said. "I'll see if you're right, and if living heirs would have to make restitution."

"Thank you."

Jason dropped her off at her house, promising to pick her up tomorrow so they could go back to Winter's Edge to collect her car in the morning.

As Wilma took off her coat, something fell onto the floor. It was a foil-covered sphere. As she bent closer, she gasped. It was another chocolate egg.

CHAPTER SIX

THE NEXT MORNING, Wilma woke early. She puttered around her modest little cottage, enjoying the solitude of a winter morning. As she went through her mail from yesterday, she found a return letter from a publisher. It was a reply about the book Jacob had helped her with. Her heart started to race as she opened it—only to stop when she heard Detective Fellow shift on the living room couch.

Last night, as soon as she found the chocolate egg, she had called him. He collected the egg and had it dusted for prints and tested for poison. Both came back negative.

"It's still a warning, Miss Wade," he said, and decided he would stay the night.

Wilma hid the letter. Whether it was good new or bad news, she would rather learn what the answer was alone. She made a pot of coffee and started making a breakfast of eggs and pancakes.

Jason emerged into the kitchen shortly after, not nearly as rumpled as one might expect. He smiled in greeting to Wilma and set the table while Wilma cooked breakfast. "We should head back to Winter's Edge today. I talked with our legal department last night, and there were several large thefts that were traced back to the family that owned the estate right before the police shut them down. There are also rumors that the missing son went on to continue the criminal empire, only more subtly than his predecessors."

"We still don't have proof that Norman is connected to the family, though," Wilma said, frowning. "And if he is, we don't have any proof that he knew it."

Jason nodded as he sat down to the plate Wilma served him. "Without a confession, it's not much good."

Wilma started cutting her pancakes, deep in thought. "Did you check the cameras to see if anyone else went into the kitchen?"

"I did. Norman was the only person there. The footprints that you found in the secret passage fit the shoes he was wearing. I haven't had the chance to ask him about it yet. I wanted to have more proof to bring against him before I did," Jason explained.

"Anne, David, and Rosie all went into the library. Rosie found him dead. Unless David and Anne are in it together, then Anne for sure is innocent. David knew about the passage to the speakeasy. Norman was in the second passage." Wilma chewed on her pancake as she considered the conundrum. The unfortunate truth of the matter was that there just wasn't any physical evidence that would prove any of their suspects did it.

Jason seemed to have the same line of thought. "Let's look at motive. Rosie and Jacob were involved. They could have had a lover's quarrel that got out of hand. David didn't approve of his daughter and Jacob and could have poisoned him to keep him away from Rosie. Anne... has no motive, really."

"Anne is looking less and less like a suspect," Wilma agreed. "Now, there's Norman. He used to live near Jacob and they didn't get along, and it's possible that he has a connection with the original family..."

"What is it, Wilma?" Jason asked, straightening.

"How did David know about the speakeasy? Did he say Jacob told him?" Wilma asked.

Jason leaned back in his chair. "He didn't say... I think we should go have a chat with David Reardon."

———

Several hours later, they were at Norman Prose's house with all the answers they needed—except for one. Wilma's heart pounded with nerves and excitement. Norman narrowed his eyes at the two of them when he saw them standing on his doorstep.

"What are you doing here?" he asked.

Detective Jason Fellow looked him in the eye. "Two weeks ago, Jacob Howell called you. He told you that he found a connection between Winter's Edge and you. Your grandfather was part of the original crime family that lived there. When the police raided and arrested the rest of them, he escaped. He didn't come back to Barwick, but he rebuilt his crime empire with everything he took with him."

Norman's jaw clenched. "What makes you think that?"

"We have Jacob's notes," Wilma answered. "What's more, you might have thought that conversation was private, but it wasn't. David Reardon overheard your conversation, including when Jacob told you about the speakeasy and the bottles of liquor inside. He heard it all. That's how he knew about the speakeasy."

Norman folded his arms. "Alright. Fine, he told me. But he never told me about how to get into the speakeasy. You can't prove I went through it to get to the library."

"We have your footprints in the dust," Wilma pointed out.

"You have footprints that match my shoes. The same shoes that half the men in the department wear. You can't prove those are my prints. They could have been left there ages before the tour," Norman said with a shrug.

Jason shook his head. "Perhaps, yes. But when we consider the video footage, we have a much more interesting situation emerge. You see, after Detective Harper left the library, she went to the kitchen. There, she made a video call with her sister in Pennsylvania. The funny thing is, she says you weren't there."

Wilma tapped her chin thoughtfully. "But the footage shows that you went into the kitchen before her, and didn't come back out until after. So where were you?"

Norman's face paled.

"Your grandfather told you about the speakeasy. He told you how to get in and out through the library and kitchen. You benefited directly from his crimes, and you hoped to be able to take and sell off everything he left behind when he fled," Wilma said.

"The only thing we can't figure out is why Jacob had to die," Jason said. "Tell us what happened and we'll talk to the DA for you."

Norman closed his eyes and let out a heavy breath. "Jacob Howell did call me. He found the speakeasy and everything in it. He put together my grandfather's connection with the house. I tried to get him to keep it quiet, wanted him to stay out of the speakeasy until I could get what should have belonged to me. I wasn't even trying to take the estate, though it should be mine. I didn't want to get mixed up in all that."

"But Jacob didn't go for that, did he?" Wilma asked.

Norman shook his head. "I heard him telling Rosie to meet him in the library. I knew he was going to share the speakeasy with her. Then where would that leave me? I wouldn't have the chance to get those bottles out, or dig up the gold."

Wilma's eyes widened. "Gold?"

"You didn't know about that?" Norman smirked. "I guess that's one thing Jacob didn't find out. Figures. He always thought he was smarter than he was. Yes. There is gold buried beneath the speakeasy. Enough to set up my retirement. I was going to go to Rio, or the Riviera. But I wasn't going to be able to get at it if Jacob told everyone about it. So, I had to act fast. I went through the kitchen up to the library." Norman let out a heavy sigh as he ran a hand through his hair. "I played it off as though it was a lucky coincidence. Got that rat talking about his planned restorations. When he wasn't looking, I put the poison in his glass. Then I just... slipped away."

A chill stole down Wilma's spine. "So, what you're saying is that you didn't come to the tour with the intention of killing him?"

"No," Norman said.

Jason moved a little closer to Wilma. "Then why did you have the poison?"

"I think you know why," Norman said, his eyes directly on Wilma.

Wilma shuddered. "So, you're the one that poisoned the egg. You're the one that stole it from the evidence locker and gave it to me again last night. Why? Why did you want to kill me?"

Norman gazed at her coldly. "It's quite simple. Those criminal activities my grandfather was involved in? My father was involved, too. I was too for a time, when I was younger. I escaped that life and rebuilt myself here in Barwick. I thought I left it all behind me."

"You thought Wilma might uncover it?" Jason asked doubtfully.

"Last year, you started to write a book," Norman said. "A book with a setting based on Winter's Edge. After the way you've solved so many cases here in Barwick, I knew that if you got too close, you'd figure out the truth. It was nothing personal. I just had to make sure you wouldn't solve the case of the missing heir."

Wilma shivered as Jason arrested Norman Prose. So, there he was. The man who tried to kill her—not for something she had done, but something she potentially could do.

And if he hadn't decided to kill Jacob, she might have been the one dead.

But it was over now. Jason pushed Norman into the cruiser.

Jacob's killer was found and she could finally be free of this fear lingering over her head.

It was over.

It was really over.

CHAPTER SEVEN

WILMA WADE STROLLED beneath the twinkling holiday lights winding up streetlight poles and trees in Centennial Park. It had been a whirlwind of a day and Wilma enjoyed the quiet of winter as snow started to fall softly. She was bundled up against the cold, enjoying the way her breath puffed out into the air. Detective Jason Fellow walked beside her, the two of them arm-in-arm.

"I always forget how beautiful winter is," Jason mused. "I think it might be my favorite season."

"Didn't you say that fall was your favorite season when the leaves were turning? And when the sunflowers were in bloom, summer was your favorite," Wilma teased with a smile.

Jason laughed. "And I do love spring. What can I say? I just love living in Barwick."

Now that the case of the poisoned Easter egg was over, Wilma felt like she could breathe deeply for the first time in months. She hadn't realized how much the fear was invading her life until now, when it was over. It still shocked her that a police detective could have been behind all of this.

"It's something of a compliment, you know," she said aloud.

"What is?"

"Norman's attempts on my life. It means he saw me as a real threat," Wilma quipped.

Jason laughed out loud. "Well, I'm not going to lie. He was right. You've been able to solve a lot of strange cases. Look at the Douglas Creel case. I mean, it was very odd but you managed to find all the clues. Then there was the Easter murder, and the case with the exotic animal trafficking. Remember the time when you were framed for murder?"

"Oh, I remember." Wilma shook her head at the memories.

"Barwick should put up a plaque for you," Jason joked.

Wilma laughed. "Don't sell yourself short. You were there every step of the way. If I should get a plaque, you should too."

"Just put me on as a footnote on yours," Jason said. "But I must admit, I'm glad it's over. I've been wondering if Detective Harper is right and I should stop bringing you into cases."

"I don't know if you have much choice on that," Wilma joked.

The wind picked up, making them both shiver. They hurried across the street to a cozy little café, where Jason ordered a burger and Wilma got a bowl of clam chowder. As they ate, warming up, Wilma remembered something she hadn't shared with Jason yet. Was this the right time? She didn't want to seem as though she was bragging after the way he praised her.

Jason saw her expression and lifted an eyebrow. "Miss Wade, you look like you have something to say."

Wilma flushed, then grinned. "You remember that book that I had Jacob help me research?"

"Yes."

"I got a letter back from a publisher about it. It's been picked up! All I have to do is sign the contract and send it back. Then, in a year or two, I'll be on bookshelves," Wilma said.

Jason grinned. "Congratulations! You deserve it. But... will it really take two years?"

"It might. Traditional publishing takes time," Wilma explained.

"Ah, I see. You know..." Jason folded his hands on the table. "We should celebrate. Both of us have done a lot this year. You're going to go spend Christmas with your cousin Martha, right?"

Wilma nodded. "Yes. She always goes more elaborate than I care for, but she's been lonely since her husband died. All her children are spending the holidays with their in-laws and rather than cause trouble, she asked if I'd come stay with her."

"Then in the New Year, why don't you and I go to Fletcher Lake Lodge. I used to go there all the time with my parents. No mystery, no danger. Just hot chocolate, skating on a frozen lake, and maybe some skiing." Jason grinned, looking exciting. "Just space to breathe."

Wilma's eyes filled with grateful tears. She understood what this meant for Jason, inviting her to a place where he went with his family. Since the first case they worked together, they had only grown closer over time. Now she reached across the table and gripped his hand tightly in hers.

"Thank you, Jason. I would love to join you at this lodge. You know that I've never had children of my own. But I have come to see you like a son," she told him, choking on her emotions.

Jason patted her hand, returning her smile. "And I'm honored to have you as an honorary mother, Wilma. You truly are a special person."

The snow kept falling outside but inside the café, it was warm and cozy. With the year drawing to an end, and another mystery solved, Wilma enjoyed the reflections on the past year and considered what she would do in the coming year. A book deal. It was what she wanted.

"This," she told Jason, "was a great year."

The End

Did you enjoy Wilma Wade Mysteries, Volume 2?

Please consider rating it on Goodreads, Bookbub, or your favorite retailer. Reviews help me reach new readers.

This concludes the **Wilma Wade Mysteries.** Turn the page to find a new series to read or join my Newsletter for writing updates, sales and promotions!

ALSO BY DAISY LANDISH

Clean Regency Romance

The Lady Series - The Allington Collection

The Lady Series - The Gillingham Collection

The Lady Series - The Blackmore Collection

The Lady Series - The Norrington Collection

Clean Contemporary Romance

Timeline Retreats - Romcom

Maplewood Grove Series - Small Town

Love on Spruce Island

Second Chance

Cherry Tree Island

The Wedding Trio

Extra Credit

Counting on the Cowboy

Focusing on the Cowboy

Mistletoe Magic

Grounded at Christmas

Cozy Mysteries

Sophie Brooks Mysteries

Jane and Kennedy Daniels Mysteries

Pine Grove Mysteries

Annie Archer Paranormal Mysteries

Wilma Wade Holiday Mysteries

Mike and Maddie Mysteries

Mystic Moonhaven Mysteries

Sweater Weather: Cozy Mysteries for Fall

Summer Vibes: Cozy Mysteries for Summer

Let it Snow: Cozy Mysteries for Winter

Spring Break: Cozy Mysteries for Spring

ABOUT THE AUTHOR

Daisy Landish is a clean romance and cozy mystery author whose clean and sweet novellas have tugged at readers' heartstrings around the world. When she's not writing love stories, Daisy spends her time reading, hiking at dawn, and riding into the sunset on her horse, Rosebud.

Join Daisy's Newsletter for updates and giveaways!
www.daisylandishromance.com

facebook.com/daisylandishromance

x.com/daisy_landish

instagram.com/daisylandishbooks

amazon.com/author/daisylandish

bookbub.com/authors/daisy-landish

goodreads.com/Daisy_Landish